10

Ch

D0914946

# THE
# CATTLEMAN'S
# ADOPTED FAMILY

# THE
# CATTLEMAN'S
# ADOPTED FAMILY

BY

BARBARA HANNAY

PORTSMOUTH PUBLIC LIBRARY
601 COURT STREET
PORTSMOUTH, VA 23704

MILLS & BOON®

All the characters in this book have no existence outside the imagination of the author, and have no relation whatsoever to anyone bearing the same name or names. They are not even distantly inspired by any individual known or unknown to the author, and all the incidents are pure invention.

All Rights Reserved including the right of reproduction in whole or in part in any form. This edition is published by arrangement with Harlequin Enterprises II BV/S.à.r.l. The text of this publication or any part thereof may not be reproduced or transmitted in any form or by any means, electronic or mechanical, including photocopying, recording, storage in an information retrieval system, or otherwise, without the written permission of the publisher.

® and TM are trademarks owned and used by the trademark owner and/or its licensee. Trademarks marked with ® are registered with the United Kingdom Patent Office and/or the Office for Harmonisation in the Internal Market and in other countries.

First published in Great Britain 2010
Large Print edition 2010
Harlequin Mills & Boon Limited,
Eton House, 18-24 Paradise Road,
Richmond, Surrey TW9 1SR

© Barbara Hannay 2010

ISBN: 978 0 263 21225 9

Harlequin Mills & Boon policy is to use papers that are natural, renewable and recyclable products and made from wood grown in sustainable forests. The logging and manufacturing process conform to the legal environmental regulations of the country of origin.

Printed and bound in Great Britain
by CPI Antony Rowe, Chippenham, Wiltshire

# PROLOGUE

AT FIRST, when Amy saw two policemen at the ballroom's grand entrance, she felt no more than mild curiosity. She didn't dream they were about to turn her life upside down.

She was way too excited to entertain such dark thoughts. For weeks, she'd been on tenterhooks planning tonight's high-gloss corporate launch. Its success or failure rested almost entirely on her shoulders, and she was relieved that everything was turning out well.

'Love it, love it, love it!' her ecstatic clients cheered.

As far as they were concerned, Amy hadn't put a foot wrong. They were thrilled with the venue she'd found on Melbourne's Southbank. They were especially thrilled with the video walls that showed off their brilliant new range of environmentally friendly lighting systems.

Amy was equally pleased with the way she looked tonight. She'd dieted for three weeks to squeeze into her divinely chic, but frighteningly expensive little black dress. She'd paid another outrageous sum at a trendy salon in Chapel Street to have glamorous blonde highlights added to her rather ordinary, pale brown hair.

Now, with the addition of killer high heels and her grandmother's diamond earrings, she'd received oodles of compliments about both the launch party and her appearance. Tonight it was clear—in Melbourne's competitive, pressure-cooker world of marketing and corporate events, Amy Ross had *arrived*!

But before she could take her first celebratory sip of her champagne cocktail, she saw the deepening sombreness on the policemen's faces.

Why on earth were they here?

Surely they must have come to the wrong function. At any moment they would move on.

But no, the older of the two men approached

the doorman and Amy saw the look of concern on his face. She felt a cold ripple of anxiety. Hastily, she scanned the crowded ballroom, searching the sea of guests. Could a criminal be lurking in their midst?

Her stomach tightened as she glanced to the doorway again. The doorman was turning.

He pointed directly at Amy.

*Oh, God.*

The glass in her hand shook, spilling wine onto her gorgeous new dress. Dismayed, she set it down. Any second now, the policemen would come marching into the very centre of this ballroom, and she had visions of the guests falling silent, eyes agog as they stepped aside to make a wide path for the blue uniformed men.

Amy knew she mustn't let that happen.

Sending her clients a brave thumbs-up gesture, she started off across the vast expanse of highly polished floor, knees knocking, thoughts racing and skidding through distressing possibilities.

Had she accidentally invited one of Melbourne's infamous gangland criminals to this party?

Or was this personal? Was *she* the policemen's target? Had her car been towed away?

Had something happened to her parents? *Please, no!*

Her stomach gave another sickening lurch as she drew closer to the grim-faced men, but she forced a smile. 'Good evening, gentlemen. How can I help you?'

The older policeman nodded to her gravely. 'Are you Miss Amy Ross?'

'Yes.'

'You live at Unit 42, 67 Grange Street, Kew?'

'Y-yes.' *Oh, cringe.* Had she forgotten to turn off the iron? Had her flat burned down?

'We've been informed that you organised this event and sent out the invitations. Is that correct?'

Amy gulped. 'That's right.'

'Could we speak with you privately, please?'

She couldn't hide her alarm any longer. 'W-what's the matter?'

'We're making enquiries, Miss Ross. We don't want to cause any unnecessary fuss, so, if you could just come this way, please?'

*Enquiries*. Surely this was a euphemism to cover all kinds of awfulness?

Stomach churning, Amy followed the men out into the marbled splendour of the hotel's lobby. She felt too ill to ask questions, so she stood very still while the younger policeman drew a piece of paper from his pocket.

She recognised it as one of the invitations she'd sent out for the launch party. Was she about to be quizzed about her guest list?

Amy's mind whirled. Her clients had vetted her guest list and her only addition had been her best friend, Rachel. It was all above board. She'd been allocated one private guest and although her initial choice had been Dominic, her boyfriend, she'd changed her mind at the last moment and invited Rachel instead.

Rachel had been her best friend since they were fifteen, and she really understood how BIG this night was.

Besides, Rachel was a single mum and a writer, and since her daughter's birth she hardly ever got out. This party was a terrific chance for her to exercise her social skills before her first book was published and she became famous.

Amy had no doubt that her brilliant friend would become famous. Of course, she wasn't surprised that Rachel was running late tonight—she'd probably had trouble leaving Bella with a babysitter.

The policeman tapped the invitation with a long finger. 'Are you the same Amy Ross who's listed as Rachel Tyler's next of kin?'

A strangled cry broke from Amy. She tried not to think the worst, but she was gripped by numb terror.

'I—I suppose Rachel might have named me as her n-next of kin,' she stammered. 'She has no family and I'm her b-best friend.'

'Your name came up when we checked her driver's licence,' the policeman said gently. Too gently.

Shaking, Amy wished with all her heart that she didn't have to hear what these men had come to tell her.

'We found this invitation and realised you'd be here,' he said.

Amy almost screamed. She wanted these men to go. Away. Right now.

Instead they were beating around the bush, driving her insane with terror. 'Please,' she sobbed. 'Just—tell me.'

'There's been an accident,' the older man said. 'A fatal accident. Only a block away.'

# CHAPTER ONE

AMY stood at the open window of the shabby hotel room in Far North Queensland, and watched a utility truck emerge out of the heat haze to the north. She felt an anxious flutter tremble from her stomach to her chest. The driver was almost certainly Seth Reardon.

Her hair was damp against the back of her neck and her cotton clothing stuck to her skin, but as the ute rattled down the street and came to a halt directly opposite the pub she wasn't sure if her discomfort was caused by the tropical heat or her nervousness.

The driver's door opened and, with an excessive lack of haste, a man unfurled from the cabin.

His build was tall and lean, a perfect match for his faded jeans and well-worn riding boots. He wore a milk-blue cotton shirt, with long sleeves rolled to his elbows to reveal sun-darkened skin on his forearms. His hair was very black.

From this angle, Amy couldn't see his face, but he crossed the empty street with a slow and easy stride that commanded attention.

Without warning, he looked up.

And saw her.

*Gulp.*

She swung away from the window, her heart thumping strangely. She'd gained a fleeting impression of masculine strength, of a grim mouth and a proud and resolute jaw, and eyes that were a breathtaking vivid blue.

'Oh, Bella,' Amy whispered, sending a glance back to the two-year-old playing with a toy pig on the bed. 'This man is your daddy.'

It was too late to change her mind, but suddenly, for the first time since she'd left Melbourne, Amy wondered if she'd done the right thing to come all this way.

Rachel had been so cagey about Bella's father. She'd always confided in Amy—*always*—and yet she hadn't breathed a word about Seth Reardon until Bella's second birthday.

Rachel had finally made the big confession after the birthday party, a very casual gathering in her backyard—a few playgroup mums and toddlers, with colourful cupcakes, jelly oranges and chocolate frogs.

Afterwards, Amy had helped to wash coffee cups and once Bella had been tucked into bed she and Rachel had opened a bottle of wine and made spaghetti. They'd eaten on the back patio and talked long into the night.

When Amy brought up the subject of Bella's father, Rachel groaned. 'Do you always have to act like my conscience?'

'But Bella's two years old now,' Amy protested. 'And she's such a gorgeous little thing. I can't help thinking there's a guy out there who's missing out on so much by not knowing her.'

To Amy's surprise, Rachel actually agreed.

'You're right,' she said, and, after almost three years of silence, the confession tumbled out.

Rachel had met this absolutely amazing guy

when she'd been working on a cattle property on Cape York, in Far North Queensland.

'I suppose I was totally overawed by him,' she admitted. 'He was the most attractive man I've ever met.'

'You mean,' Amy whispered, 'he was *The One*?'

Rachel's face was white, her voice edgy. 'Yes, I'm afraid he was—but that's what scared me, Ames. That's why I never kept in touch with him. If I'd told him about Bella, he would have wanted me to live up there with him.'

'But if you love each other you'd live happily ever after,' Amy declared. It seemed incredibly simple and romantic to her.

But Rachel's mask slipped to reveal raw fear. 'I couldn't live there,' she said. 'He's the boss of a massive cattle station. It occupies his whole life, and it's so hot and wild and remote. I'd be mad with loneliness and I'd drive the poor man insane.'

A glass of wine later Rachel said more calmly, 'You're right, Amy. God help me, you're always right. I really must make contact with Seth again.

I do want to take Bella to meet him. I just need to find the right time.'

But she'd never found the right time…

Which was why Amy was here now, in the Tamundra pub, almost three thousand kilometres north of Melbourne.

When Seth Reardon heard footsteps on the bare timber stairs, he stood in the empty hotel dining room, facing the doorway, shoulders squared, hands lightly fisted at his sides.

He wasn't looking forward to meeting this friend of Rachel Tyler's, and he frowned, sensing something odd as he listened to Amy Ross's approach.

He was here for a business meeting and he'd expected to meet her alone, but he could hear another set of footsteps—eager, small footsteps.

Without warning, a tiny girl burst, like a small torpedo, through the doorway.

'Hello, man!'

Arms outstretched, the child greeted Seth with a huge grin, as if a reclusive cattleman, whom she'd never met, was the one person in the world she most wanted to see.

Seth's stomach dropped as she headed straight for his knees, blue eyes dancing, dark curls bouncing. He knew next to nothing about children, would rather face an angry scrub bull than a small, toddling female.

To his relief, an anxious young woman, the same woman he'd glimpsed in the window upstairs—Amy Ross, he presumed—came hurrying behind the child.

'Bella!' She reached for the little girl's hand and halted her headlong dash to embrace Seth's legs.

'I'm sorry,' she huffed, slightly out of breath and blushing brightly. 'I'm afraid Bella's very friendly.'

'So I see.'

Seth's dryly drawled response was the result of habit rather than displeasure. Now that the child was safely perched on her mother's hip, he could see that the two of them formed a charming picture.

The child's dark, curly hair, dimples, and blue eyes were in startling contrast to her mother's brown eyes and straight honey-brown hair. Amy

Ross's complexion was warmer than her daughter's, with the slightest hint of a golden tan.

But in spite of the differences in their appearances, the close bond between the two of them was clear, and Seth was suddenly lassoed by unexpected emotion. He'd been stoically resigned to his life as a loner, but now he felt strangely left out, excluded from a very special unit.

He'd thought he'd thrown off his urges to be a family man.

'Perhaps we should start again,' Amy Ross said, and she held out her hand with a smile as appealing as her daughter's. 'I'm Amy and you must be Seth. How do you do?'

He accepted her greeting with a stiff nod, and as they shook hands he was super-conscious of the soft warmth of her skin.

'You didn't mention that you were bringing your daughter,' he said with an asperity he immediately regretted.

Amy's eyes widened. 'I hope you don't mind. I'm afraid I couldn't leave Bella behind. She's usually well behaved.'

Seth made no comment and the little girl continued to regard him with enormous delight, which he found quite extraordinary.

He swallowed to clear the tightening in his throat. He was mad with himself for allowing a total stranger—a woman, no less—to convince him to drop everything and race into town.

Admittedly, Amy Ross's phone call had delivered alarming news that Seth couldn't afford to ignore. He'd been shocked to hear about Rachel Tyler's death. He hadn't heard from Rachel since she'd worked on Serenity, and he'd tried to put her clear out of his mind.

Her death was a tragedy.

And already, there'd been too much tragedy.

Amy hooked the straps of her shoulder bag more securely and held Bella's hand. But the child immediately began to squirm.

'Man, up!' she demanded, running to Seth's side and tugging at his denim jeans with determined little hands.

'Bella, no.' Grimacing with embarrassment, Amy pulled picture books from her shoulder bag. 'Come and sit here quietly and look at these books while I talk to Mr Reardon. Come on now, be a good girl.'

Seth tried to be patient while Bella was persuaded to sit cross-legged on the carpeted floor with books and a handful of toys. He and Amy sat at one of the dining tables.

'Hey, diddle, diddle,' the child announced gleefully.

He stifled a sigh of irritation. 'Does your daughter usually accompany you to business meetings, Mrs Ross?'

'Cat an' fiddle,' chanted Bella.

Flushing, Amy nervously lifted her hair from the back of her neck. Clearly, the heat and the tropical humidity were bothering her. Her hair was damp against her skin, and her neck was flushed and shiny with perspiration.

'I'm not married,' she said.

It was only then, as Seth watched her elegant hands securing a twist in her honey hair, that he noticed she wasn't wearing rings.

So she was a single mother. He supposed he

should be more tolerant. He'd heard all the news reports about the excessive costs of day care.

'I don't usually have Bella with me while I'm working,' she said. 'But I had to travel such a long way this time, and I didn't want to leave her.'

He bit back a question about the child's father, but he couldn't help wondering where the guy was and why he hadn't been able or willing to help out.

'You've come quite a distance,' he said.

'Don't I know it? It's so hot and muggy here.' She lifted the limp collar of her cotton shirt away from her skin. 'The tourist agency told me it's as far from Melbourne to Tamundra as it is from London to Moscow.'

Seth nodded. 'And you've chosen the very worst time of the year to make such a long journey.'

Her lower lip pouted. 'I had no choice. There's so little time to get publicity organised. Rachel's book is coming out in April.'

'Ah, yes, Rachel Tyler's book,' Seth said quietly and he narrowed his eyes.

'Aren't you pleased about it?'

'Why should I be pleased? When Rachel was on Serenity three years ago, she never once mentioned to anyone that she planned to write a book. I was very sorry to hear about her accident, but I can't say I'm happy that there's a book coming out now, after such a long silence.'

'Rachel's—Rachel was—a brilliant writer. She had a wonderful gift for description.'

That was all very well, but what had she described? As a reclusive bachelor, who prized his privacy, Seth was distinctly unhappy that a former employee had written a book about the six weeks she'd spent on his cattle property.

On the phone last week, Amy Ross had gone to great lengths to assure him that the book was a work of fiction and people's names had been changed to protect the innocent. But Seth wasn't at all confident he could assume that Rachel Tyler had been discreet.

Rachel had claimed to have been on a backpacking holiday, but she'd never hinted that she planned to race off and write a book about it.

To Seth, Rachel's behaviour had been sneaky.

People in the bush were upfront and open and the whole business of this book made his gut churn with apprehension. Even so, he was determined to find out what he could. It was why he'd agreed to this meeting.

He frowned at Amy. 'You were Rachel's best friend, so I assume you can shed some light on this book.'

Amy smiled awkwardly. 'I'm afraid I don't know much at all. I'm here because the publishers have a limited budget for the promotion, and I wanted to do as much as I could for—for—'

Her eyes rested on the child. 'I wanted to do this for Rachel.'

The little girl looked up suddenly. 'Mummy?'

To Seth's surprise, Amy paled and closed her eyes, as if the child had upset her.

When she opened her eyes again, a moment later, Seth was struck by their dark, liquid beauty.

There was something very graceful and feminine about Amy Ross that he found eminently watchable. On the other hand, there was something about her story that didn't quite add up.

The child's presence…Amy's nervousness… Her insistence on coming now at such an inappropriate time when the wet season was about to break over their heads.

He knew Amy hoped to return to Serenity with him to take publicity shots, but already he was convinced that even agreeing to this meeting had been a huge mistake.

Amy could feel her heart beating in her throat. It had been such a shock to see Seth and Bella together. She'd never dreamed there could be such a strong likeness between a grown man and a baby girl, and she found it hard to believe that he hadn't seen the resemblance for himself.

How much time did she have before he began to notice and to ask difficult, searching questions?

She was pretty sure he could see huge holes in her claim that she'd come here solely to gather promotional material for Rachel's book. She was terrified Seth Reardon might change his mind about allowing her to spend a couple of days on his cattle property, and if that happened she would have no choice but to reveal her real reason for coming north.

But she couldn't tell him yet.

It was too soon.

To surprise this cold and forbidding cattleman with the news that he'd fathered a daughter was a delicate and difficult exercise. The timing was crucial, and there was no way she wanted to tell him such distressing news now in this strange hotel, miles from anywhere.

This exercise couldn't be rushed. She needed a chance to get to know Seth Reardon first. She wanted to win his confidence and trust—if that were possible, which right now she seriously doubted. She had hoped that together she and Seth could work out the best way to care for her precious Bella.

Amy forced a shaky smile, uncomfortably conscious that Seth Reardon was an exceptionally good-looking man. Rachel had always had good taste in men, and Seth's lean, rugged physique and arresting blue eyes were enough to make any young woman forget her mother's warnings.

Last night, when Amy had arrived here, she'd mentioned his name to the publican's wife, Marie, and the woman's reaction had puzzled her.

'Seth Reardon?' Her eyes had widened with sudden surprise. 'Oooh… He's a quiet one. Doesn't hang around the pub much. He's…cold. But there's something about him though. Eyes that make you wonder.'

'Wonder what?' Amy had prompted, hoping to hear a positive comment.

The woman had actually blushed, and then she'd shot a quick glance at Bella, who'd been sitting at the dining table, absorbed in drinking a glass of iced milk with a straw.

'What?' Amy had asked again.

'Oh, I've always had a soft spot for a man with blue eyes,' Marie had said lamely and she'd become very busy clearing dishes while she muttered about needing to get back to the kitchen.

Amy had been left with the impression that Seth Reardon was dangerous.

Even Rachel had admitted that Seth had been cool and distant at first, until she'd got to know him.

Not that Amy would allow her mind to dwell on thoughts of Rachel and Seth becoming familiar…

Or intimate.

The very idea…of Seth Reardon making love…was like a close encounter with a lightning bolt.

He sent a frowning glance to the window and Amy saw that it had started to rain rather heavily. 'When you phoned last week you said you planned to take photographs, but this weather's going to rule that out. I did try to warn you that this is the wet season.'

'I suppose I could take photos of the rain. Rachel might have written about the wet season.'

'I doubt it. She was here in the dry season, in the winter.'

'Oh, yes, of course.'

Seth frowned at her. 'Haven't you read her book?'

'Actually…no.'

Her friend had been uncharacteristically protective about this story and she'd never offered Amy so much as a peek at the manuscript.

After the accident, Amy hadn't liked to search through the files on Rachel's computer. It had felt too much like snooping. She had sat down once to read a section of Rachel's poetry, but she'd been overcome by grief. It was like hearing Rachel's voice—and the thoughts expressed had been too intensely personal.

Amy had been in tears as she'd shut down the computer.

She hadn't opened it again.

Seth's eyes widened. 'How do you plan to promote this book, then?'

'These are early days, and I'm just starting my research. I have the publisher's back-cover copy, and a picture of the front cover. It's rather beautiful. Would you like to see it?'

She dug a folder out of her bag, and handed it to him. The book's cover depicted a balmy tropical beach at sunset with palm trees and white sand. Distant islands floated in the background, and the sun melted into a smooth golden sea.

'I know it's not very accurate,' she admitted, sending another glance out of the window.

She'd been dismayed by Tamundra's rather desolate main street and the drab gum trees beyond it, and red earth that stretched for miles. She was pretty sure the whole of Cape York looked just as bad, so the cover was deceptive to say the least.

Seth Reardon shrugged. 'There are sections on the eastern edge of Serenity that look exactly like that.'

'Oh.' Amy looked again at the idyllic palm trees and golden sand and felt her jaw drop with surprise.

Seth's blue eyes froze her. 'You haven't done your homework, Amy Ross.'

'I—I've done my best,' she spluttered. 'I—I told you I've only just started. It's only two months since Rachel died and I—I've been busy. With Bella.'

They both looked down at Bella, who was sprawled on the carpet, busy with a scrapbook and fat crayons.

'My drawing Amy,' the little girl announced proudly as she made a lopsided circle with a purple crayon. 'An' here's Amy's eyes.'

Happily, Bella drew small purple squiggles inside the circle.

Amy gave her an encouraging smile. 'That's lovely, Bella. Now draw my mouth.'

A small sigh escaped Seth and he lifted his gaze from the child and studied Amy.

She resisted an urge to squirm beneath his scrutiny. It was important to appear calm and in control.

'I'd like to know more about Rachel's stay up here,' she said, hoping to convince Seth that she wasn't wasting his time. 'What kind of work was she doing? How did she fit into life on a cattle station?'

To her dismay, his frown deepened. With a long brown finger he tapped the book's back cover blurb. 'But the answers to your questions are right here.'

'They're generalities,' she countered, desperately trying to ignore the niggling of her conscience that told her he was right. 'I'm looking for details.'

His expression was immediately guarded. 'What kind of details?'

Amy gulped. 'Nothing too personal.'

His frown deepened and she felt her face redden.

'I'm looking for anything quirky or interesting,' she said. 'Rachel was a city girl. I doubt she'd ever touched a cow before she came here, or cooked on an open fire, or slept in a swag on the ground.'

Abruptly, Seth stood, making his chair scrape on the wooden floor. He strode to the window, where he leaned a shoulder against the wall, looking out into the rain as he thrust his hands into his jeans pockets.

'I'm afraid you've wasted your time.'

'What do you mean?' She knew she sounded too scared, but was he going to refuse to take her to Serenity?

Seth's eyes narrowed. 'If you've come all this way in search of scandal to spice up the promotion, you should leave now,' he said.

'Scandal?' Amy was dumbfounded. 'Why would I want to tarnish my best friend's name?'

'For money? To sell more books? You're in marketing, aren't you?'

'How dare you?'

Seth shrugged again. 'Whatever. But you haven't been straight with me.'

Oh, help. Already he was pushing her towards making her confession. But if she told him about his daughter now, he might be so immediately shocked and angry that he stormed back to his cattle station alone, without giving her a chance to really discuss what was best for Bella.

'Rachel was my best friend,' Amy told him, softly. 'And—and I've lost her.'

She tried to go on, but suddenly the difficult, grief-filled weeks since Rachel's death seemed to overwhelm her. It had been a nightmare trying to deal with the horror of her best friend's death while taking on the responsibility of her little daughter.

She'd been trying so hard to do everything right, including coming all this way.

Now, on the brink of failure, Amy couldn't look at Seth, didn't want him to see her tears.

'Look,' he said suddenly, clearly uncomfortable with her evident emotion, 'I'm prepared to take your word.'

Her head snapped up.

Grimly, he said, 'But if you're coming to Serenity with me, we'd better get cracking, before this weather really sets in.'

Her jaw dropped, she was so surprised by his sudden hasty about-face.

'Did you drive here from Cairns?' he asked brusquely.

Amy blinked. 'Yes. I hired a car.'

'A small sedan?'

'Yes.'

'With four-wheel-drive capability?'

She shook her head.

'You'd better travel in my vehicle, then,' he said quietly and with grim resignation.

Seth was actually offering her a lift. Was it wise to accept? Would he also be willing to drive her back here in two days' time?

'Wouldn't it be simpler if I followed you in my car?' she said.

'The road's too rough and in this rain it'll be

slippery. I don't want you or your little daughter's safety on my conscience. But let's not waste time. It's a long drive.'

# CHAPTER TWO

SETH wasn't exaggerating his desire for a hasty departure.

Fortunately, Bella didn't kick up a fuss when she was suddenly strapped into a booster seat in the back of his dual-cabin ute. The little girl was mildly puzzled, but she'd lunched on Vegemite and cheese sandwiches, a banana and milk, so she obligingly fell asleep soon after they left Tamundra.

Rain streamed down the windows, making the sky and the trees a grey blur. Amy could see nothing but a small view, cleared by the wipers, of the muddy red track in front of the vehicle.

Apparently it would be dark by the time they got to Seth's property, but despite the prospect of a long journey he didn't seem inclined to talk.

Whenever Amy stole a glance his way, he looked utterly relaxed and competent, his sun-browned hands resting lightly on the steering wheel as he skilfully negotiated the rough and slippery surface.

Amy supposed he would look equally relaxed and competent on the back of a horse, or driving a tractor.

She was surprised that she wasn't more worried about heading into the wilderness with a man she hardly knew. Seth Reardon was different from almost any man she'd ever met, and she could totally understand how Rachel had been both attracted to him, and cautious about sharing her life with him.

He was clearly at ease in his own skin, but he had the wary intelligence of a loner—the Outback equivalent of street smarts, she supposed. More than likely, he never allowed anyone to get too close, which meant it wasn't going to be easy to find the right moment to tell him that Bella was his daughter.

And yet, the weight of her secret loomed large. She would be relieved to finally get it off her chest.

Needing to make conversation, she asked tentatively, 'Have you lived here on Cape York all your life?'

Seth shook his head. 'I moved up here when I was twelve.'

Amy waited for him to expand on this and when he didn't, she dived in with more questions. It was ridiculous to waste this golden opportunity for a getting-to-know-you chat.

'Where did you live before that?'

'In Sydney.'

'Really?'

'Does that surprise you?' he asked, sliding a quick glance her way.

'I was expecting you to say that you moved here from another cattle property in Queensland.' Bustling, metropolitan Sydney was as alien to this environment as her own home in Melbourne. 'Coming here must have been a big change for you.'

Seth nodded. 'I came after my father died, to live with my uncle.'

'So it was a very big change,' Amy said quietly,

and she was unexpectedly moved by the thought of him as a grieving, lonely boy, on the cusp of adolescence, leaving his friends in the city to live so far away.

She wanted to ask him about his mother. Why hadn't she been able to look after him when his father died? Why had he been moved into an uncle's care?

A glance at the set lines in Seth's face, however, silenced further questions.

The rain continued as they drove on.

The relentless downpour and Seth's rather grim silence were enough to make Amy feel sorry for herself. It wasn't her habit to be self-pitying, but the weeks since Rachel's accident had been rough and she wasn't quite sure how she'd managed, actually.

She'd made the decision to care for Bella swiftly. On the night of the accident she'd gone to Rachel's house, numb with shock, and paid the sitter, then tiptoed into the little room where Bella lay innocently asleep.

She'd looked down at the little girl's soft,

chubby-cheeked face, at her closed eyes and her soft, dark eyelashes and her heart had almost broken.

There'd been no question. She had to devote herself to caring for Rachel's daughter. A succession of babysitters could never provide the round-the-clock security and stability a two-year-old needed.

But the transition from marketing to motherhood hadn't been easy, especially when in the midst of it all, Amy's boyfriend, Dominic, had suggested that they both needed time out...to give each other some space.

Amy had known it was the thin edge of the wedge that would crack their relationship irreparably apart. Dominic was jealous of the closeness she'd quickly developed with Bella. He'd started to snap at the little girl when she'd innocently interrupted his computer games. Being upfront as usual, Amy had told him that things had to change now that Bella had arrived.

In the end they'd had the most appallingly ugly and bitter row over Bella. Dominic couldn't see why Amy should automatically assume responsibility.

The fact that she'd been named as Bella's guardian was a mere technicality, he said. It didn't mean she had to care for the child day in, day out—which proved that, after almost twelve months together, he didn't really know Amy at all.

She'd reminded him that he was living in her house, that she always had to jog his memory to get him to pay for his share of the food, the phone and the electricity, and she'd also let him know how annoying it was when he disappeared into the spare room and spent hours on computer games, racking up a huge Internet bill as well.

Whether Dominic had left her or whether she'd finally shown him the door was academic now. The whole catastrophe had been draining, and Amy might have collapsed in a complete heap if Bella hadn't been so resilient and such an utter darling.

It was amazing how quickly the little girl had transferred her trust to Amy, and the nights when she'd cried for her mummy had gradually lessened, but it still cut Amy to the core that she was now the focus of the little girl's love, the love that rightly belonged to Rachel.

She'd get weepy, though, if she thought too much about that.

For much of the journey the vehicle rattled down a long straight track, which every so often climbed a low hill, then dipped down again to cross a rising creek. Yesterday, on her journey north to Tamundra, the creeks had been mere trickles, but already these gullies had begun to swell with fast-flowing muddy water.

Seth drove in silence and Amy felt the beginnings of a tension headache. She let her head fall back and tried again to relax as she watched the rain slide down her window. Every so often she caught the blurred outlines of cattle hunched together in mobs, looking desolate. A stalwart few continued to graze, apparently untroubled by the driving rain.

Bella woke up and was immediately chirpy and eager.

'Moo cow!' she announced importantly. And then 'Moo! Moo!' over and over.

Amy stole glances in Seth's direction and she was quietly pleased to catch him smiling at Bella's enthusiasm.

He looked incredibly gorgeous when he smiled.

Amy wondered if he'd been infatuated by Rachel. Most guys had been. Had there been other girlfriends since? She supposed there wouldn't be too many available women here in the wilderness, but perhaps there was a beautiful girl who waited impatiently in Cairns for Seth's visits.

'How long were you and Rachel friends?' Seth asked suddenly, much to Amy's surprise.

At first she was nervous that he'd guessed the direction of her thoughts, and almost as quickly she worried that he'd somehow made the link between Bella and Rachel. But he looked too relaxed, and Amy let out a huff of relief.

Actually, she was really pleased that he wanted to talk, especially to talk about Rachel. It would pave the way for the news she had to share.

'Rachel and I were both fifteen when we met,' she told him, 'and we were in hospital, having our appendixes out.'

'Ouch. I suppose you cheered each other up,' he suggested with a smile.

Heavens. A smile *and* conversation. Things were looking up.

Amy returned his smile. 'We had a great time. We were in a small hospital run by nuns and we had beds side by side in a room to ourselves. We soon discovered we were in the same year at school, so we had tons to talk about.'

'And you stayed in touch afterwards?'

She nodded. 'Rachel went to a very snobby, private girls' college and I went to an ordinary co-ed state school, so we didn't see much of each other, but we kept in email contact. And we got together on weekends sometimes. Rachel even came away with my family to the beach for the summer holidays.'

'You really clicked,' Seth said quietly.

'We did, and then we ended up at Melbourne University, and that's when we truly became best friends.'

She took a packet of butterscotch from her bag. 'Would you like one of these?'

'Thanks.'

'I'll unwrap it for you.' Carefully, she untwisted the ends of the paper and as she offered him the sweet his hand bumped hers. She felt a zap of electricity that made her gasp. *Good grief.* She shouldn't be getting the hots for this guy.

To cover the reaction she said quickly, 'I suppose you went to a boarding school.'

Seth nodded, and finished chewing before he said, 'I used to fly down to school in Townsville.'

'I've always thought boarding school would be great fun.'

'Yeah. We had plenty of fun.' He looked genuinely happy as he said this.

'And what about after school?' Amy prompted, more tentatively. 'Did you go straight back to your uncle's property?'

An almost imperceptible sigh escaped Seth. 'I spent a year in England, playing rugby.'

She was so surprised she almost cried out. She struggled to picture Seth Reardon in a rugby jersey on a soft green English playing field, sur-

rounded by his teammates. He was athletic, certainly, but was he a team player?

She'd had him pegged as a natural-born loner.
'Was it hard to come back to Cape York?'

'Not at all.'

He said this quickly, almost too quickly, and
his eyes became very bright and hard, as if he
was warding off any further discussion.

After that, they continued their journey in
silence once more, while Amy's mind seethed
with unasked questions. There were so many
gaps in Seth's story, things he plainly had no intention of sharing with her. Where was his
mother? Was she dead too? Did he miss Sydney?
Or rugby? Or England?

Most of all, she wondered if he really liked
living on Cape York. If he didn't, why had he
stayed up here in the north? If he'd been willing
to move south, he and Rachel and Bella might
have been a family.

One thing was becoming very clear to her,
however. She'd underestimated Seth Reardon.

She'd come north with the vague idea that

she'd meet a guy wearing an Akubra hat, a suntan and a smile. She'd imagined an attractive, but uncomplicated, country fellow, who'd had an affair with her best friend and who now deserved to know that the affair had resulted in…consequences.

She'd been a fool to think that it would be easy and straightforward to share the news about Bella with him.

Twisting around in her seat, she looked back at Bella, who'd dozed off again, but then woken up to gaze around the interior of the vehicle with a slightly dazed frown. Amy felt her heart swell with love for the dear, innocent little scrap.

It was hard to believe that she'd grown so close to her in two short months, but the truth was her emotional connection to Rachel's daughter was so strong at times it shocked her.

They'd been on quite a journey together, she and this little girl, as they'd slowly learned to cope with unbearable loss, and to live with each other.

To love each other.

These days, more often than not, Amy woke

when Bella bounced into her bed, eager to greet her with hugs and kisses and laughter.

With Bella, Amy had discovered the joy of simply being alive. She'd relearned the pleasure of simple things like trips to the park to feed the ducks, riding slippery slides, and splashing in wading pools. She'd forgotten that it could be so much fun to blow bubbles at bath time, or to share bedtime picture books.

Already, it was hard to remember a time when corporate launches with champagne cocktails and gourmet canapés had been vitally, crucially important.

More often than not, meal preparation these days involved oatmeal or boiled eggs and toast soldiers, and bunny-shaped mugs of milk. Amy had learned to always carry an extra bag, to accommodate Bella's sunhat and a change of clothes, as well as a drink and a banana, or tiny packets of sultanas for snacks.

Her life in marketing had been put on hold.

Being self-employed had made the transition possible—not easy, but possible—but there was a limit to how long she could continue this life-style without earning. She'd already gobbled up a major chunk of her savings. Luckily, she had no big debts hanging over her, but she knew she would have to return to work soon.

Just the same, she certainly hadn't come looking for Bella's father because she needed his financial help. Caring for Bella might require a few sacrifices, but Amy knew she would manage.

Eventually, they stopped at a gate and Seth got out to open it.

'Are we almost there?' Amy asked hopefully when he got back into the car. Bella was grizzling more loudly now. 'Is this Serenity?'

'This is one of the boundary gates,' he said as he steered the vehicle between timber fence posts. 'I'm afraid it'll be another half-hour before we reach the homestead.'

*Another half-hour…* It was already dusk, and growing dark quickly because of the rain. Amy found it hard to imagine owning so much land that you could drive across it for such a long time.

Seth got out again to shut the gate, and when

he came back he said, 'Would you like to let Bella out for a bit, to stretch her legs?'

'I'm sure she'd love that, but it's raining.'

'You have raincoats, don't you?'

'Well, yes.'

Seth shrugged. 'This is the tropics, after all. The rain's not cold.'

'You're right.' In a matter of moments, Amy found their raincoats, which she'd packed in an outside pocket of her suitcase, and she was buttoning Bella into hers. She glanced at Seth, who was standing alone…looking…not lonely, surely?

A sudden instinct prompted her to ask, 'Are you coming to walk with us?'

For the first time, Seth lost his air of cool certainty. His bright eyes rested on Bella's eager face peering up at him from beneath the yellow hood of her raincoat. The lines of his face softened, then broke into a smile.

Wow! Amy felt the impact of his smile deep in the pit of her stomach.

'Why not?' he said and he snagged a dark oilskin coat from the back of the vehicle.

Amy's chest felt weirdly tight, but moments later they set off together along the red dirt track between straggling gumtrees and pandanus palms.

Bella was thrilled to be allowed out in the rain, skipping between the two adults. She insisted on holding their hands, but every so often she would let go and dash off to splash in a puddle, then she would turn and grin at them ecstatically and Amy's heart would leap into her throat.

Surely Seth must see how closely the little girl's smile resembled his?

But apart from that anxiety, Amy enjoyed the little outing much more than she should have. There was something about being out in the rain in the middle of a journey through nowhere, just for fun, that felt impossibly rash and carefree. Seth was smiling almost the whole time and their gazes kept meeting. Every time his blue eyes met hers she felt a knife-edgy thrill zap through her.

It was inappropriate and foolish, but she couldn't help it. A strange, shiver-sweet happiness seemed to have gripped her and she felt as if she could have walked along the darkening, rain swept track for ever.

But at last she had to be sensible and to suggest that it was time to head back to the ute.

As they went on Seth had to get out to open and close gates at least another six times. Each time he got back into the car, he brought the smell of damp earth and a fine spray of rain.

'I should be looking after the gates,' Amy protested after the third stop.

'Outback gates are notoriously tricky.' He frowned as he looked at her more closely. 'Are you OK? You're looking pale.'

'Bit tired. That's all. I'm fine, thanks.' Truth was, she was feeling ill and scared, scared of the shivers of awareness this man caused. It was ridiculous to feel so hung up about him. He was Rachel's ex, and Bella's father, and once she revealed her real reason for coming here he might hate her.

'We're almost there,' he said, sounding surprisingly gentle.

Ahead of them, Amy saw lights winking

through the rain, and then at last they pulled up at the bottom of a short flight of wooden steps.

She was familiar with pictures in magazines of homesteads on Outback cattle stations—ageing timber houses with corrugated iron roofs and wrap-around verandas, sitting in the middle of grassy paddocks.

It was too dark to see much tonight, but if she guessed correctly they'd arrived at the back of this house. Rain drummed loudly on the iron roof, and the veranda was in darkness but a light came on as they got out of the vehicle.

They hung their damp coats on pegs near the back door and Seth turned to Amy. 'I'll show you straight to your room,' he said, watching her with a thoughtful frown.

'Thanks.'

He walked ahead of them, carrying their bags, and Amy followed, hugging Bella close, reassured by the familiar warmth and softness of her baby skin. She wondered where Seth's uncle was. Wondered if she should tell Seth tonight, while they were alone, that this little girl was his daughter.

Surely it was better to get the truth out in the open sooner rather than later?

Fear rippled through her as she pictured the moment of revelation. She had no idea how Seth would react, whether he would be angry, or shocked, or disbelieving. Or suspicious of her motives.

Or all of the above.

Perhaps it would be prudent to wait till the morning. It had been a long, unsettling day. Her tiredness made her fragile and susceptible to tears and she wanted to be strong like a mother lion when she broached Bella's future with this man.

'I thought this room should suit you,' Seth said, pushing open a door.

'Oh.' Amy couldn't hold back an exclamation of surprise as she entered the room and he set their bags down. 'This is lovely.'

It was the prettiest room possible, with soft, pale green carpet and matching green and cream wall-paper. Romantic mosquito nets hung over twin beds and French doors opened onto the veranda.

'There's an en-suite bathroom through there.' He pointed to a door.

'Thank you, Seth. That's wonderful.'

Setting Bella down, Amy peeped around the doorway. The bathroom was sparkling clean and as lovely as the bedroom. Thick, soft towels hung on the rails and there was even a purple orchid in a cut-glass vase on the washbasin. It was amazing, really, to find such comfort all the way out here, like coming across a mirage in the middle of a desert.

Perhaps Seth and his uncle were used to having guests. Amy wondered if he wasn't nearly as antisocial as she'd believed. This wonder was compounded when she turned back into the bedroom, and found Bella and the antisocial man in question trying to touch the ends of their noses with their tongues.

As she watched them Amy's throat tightened and her mouth wobbled dangerously. They looked so alike, giggling together and having such incredible fun being silly. Without warning, her guilty conscience got the better of her and she very nearly blurted out the truth. Right there and then, accompanied by tears.

*I mustn't. Not now. It would be too cruel to walk into Seth's house and immediately dump the news on him like an emotional thunderstorm.*

She pretended to be terribly busy, opening Bella's suitcase, struggling to feel calmer.

As if he hadn't noticed anything amiss, Seth said, 'I told Ming we'd be happy with something light for supper. How do scrambled eggs with tea and toast sound?'

'That sounds fine.' She was dazed with surprise. 'Who's Ming?'

Seth smiled. 'My cook.'

*His cook?*

Amy blinked. This was another surprise. From the way Rachel had spoken, she'd always imagined that life on this cattle station was pretty rough.

'So are scrambled eggs OK?' Seth asked.

'Yes,' she said. 'They'd be perfect. Bella would love some, too.'

'No problem. I'll let Ming know. Come along to the kitchen when you're ready. It's just down the hall.'

'One, two, five, six!' Bella chanted proudly as she counted the buttered fingers of toast on her plate, then beamed happy smiles at both Amy and Seth.

They were eating alone in the kitchen, the mysterious Ming having prepared their food and then disappeared before Amy could meet him.

Fortunately, Bella was quite adept at filling any awkward silences that lapsed during their dinnertime conversation. In between Bella's choruses, Amy answered Seth's questions about her work in marketing and he elaborated on the export beef market.

She wished she could follow up on their earlier conversation with more personal questions like how he'd felt about giving up rugby, or whether he planned to live on Cape York for ever. Or whether he looked forward to having a family one day. Most importantly, she wanted to know how he'd felt about Rachel.

Instead, she told him about her Melbourne flat and Bella's playgroup and the day care centre where she planned to leave Bella when she returned to work.

Seth's gaze met Amy's when she told him this, and wariness crept into his eyes, as if he sensed her underlying tension.

All of a sudden she was desperately, achingly tired and she realised she'd been tense for hours. The closer she got to telling Seth about his relationship to Bella, the more frightened she was.

The fact was, telling Seth was one thing. Handing her precious little girl over was another matter entirely. Amy had no intention of giving her away. As Bella's guardian, she planned to take the child back to Melbourne with her. Seth could stay in touch, certainly, but he couldn't expect to have Bella permanently.

Could he?

All through the meal, there was a question in his eyes, which Amy tried to avoid. She focused on his hands as he cut a piece of toast into the shape of a sailing boat for Bella. They were very workmanlike hands—sinewy and strong and suntanned. To Amy's intense dismay, she found herself imagining his hands on her skin and the thought caused crazy explosions deep inside.

By the end of the meal, Bella was growing sleepy again and Amy grabbed the excuse to escape, to put her to bed.

'Good idea,' Seth agreed easily, but as Amy was about to leave he said, 'Would you have time for a chat after Bella's settled?'

Time for a chat?

Her heart jumped with sudden fright. Why did his simple question sound ominous? His blue gaze was quiet and steady, in complete contrast to her hectic pulse.

'Yes, of course,' she managed to reply. 'It shouldn't take too long to settle Bella.'

'Half an hour?'

'That's plenty of time.'

For once Amy was pleased that Bella knew every word of her bedtime story by heart. She only had to turn the pages while the little girl happily pointed to the pictures and recited snippets of dialogue.

Meanwhile, Amy's mind raced, trying to guess why Seth wanted to chat.

Ever since Rachel's accident, her mind had developed the alarming habit of leaping to worst-case scenarios. She wondered if Seth wanted to talk about Rachel and Bella. Could he have guessed?

She wasn't ready to tell Seth the truth. She'd mentally prepared herself for a confession in the morning.

But would there ever be a right time?

Amy watched Bella's innocent little face as she snuggled down beneath the crisp white sheets with her favourite toy, a fat stuffed pig.

'Night, night,' she murmured, touching her fingers to a silky curl of jet-black hair.

Bella eyed her sternly. 'Say bed bugs.'

'Bossy boots,' Amy chided, but she obliged. 'Night, night, sweetheart. Don't let the bed bugs bite.'

Bella grinned with satisfaction and they hugged tightly. Amy kissed her warm, baby-soft skin, and tried not to think about distressing possibilities that involved handing Bella over, or nights in the future without this ritual.

An awful panic gripped her, and suddenly she knew with blinding clarity how vitally and deeply important Bella had become to her. She simply couldn't bear to give her up.

Sitting on the edge of the bed, she fought tears as she stroked the child's soft curls and watched her eyelids grow heavy. And she tried, frantically, to sort out a strategy in her mind for dealing with Seth Reardon.

# CHAPTER THREE

SETH stood on the back veranda, staring out into the rain without really seeing it. Instead, he kept seeing a lovely young woman and her cute little daughter, so happy together, and the image gnawed at a private pain he'd tried very hard to keep buried.

With an angry groan he strode to the far end of the veranda, and stared out into the black, rain-lashed night, willing his reckless thoughts to the four winds.

He'd invited this woman and her child into his home, and already today, during a simple walk down a bush track, he'd let down his guard. But he knew that he mustn't allow a single mother's warm brown eyes and her daughter's appealing ways to slip under his defences.

It seemed there was no other man in the picture for Amy and Bella, but so what? Seth had given up all thoughts of domestic happiness, and he'd done so with the fierce determination of a smoker, or a gambler giving up an addiction.

Women, he'd learned after too many mistakes, were a health hazard. Families looked cosy and attractive when viewed from the outside, but he knew from bitter firsthand experience that the inside story could be something else entirely.

Closing his eyes, Seth saw his own mother— slim, elegant and beautiful, her sleek, dark hair framing her face like a satin cap. He remembered her tinkling laugh and the way she'd smelled of delicate flowers. Remembered her infrequent hugs.

He remembered, too, the many evenings he'd stood, nose pressed against the glass, watching her from his bedroom window as she stepped into a limousine. She'd always looked remote, like a goddess, in a glamorous red evening gown, in sequins, or gold lamé—a glittering evening bag in one hand, cigarette in the other.

Mostly, he remembered the day she'd left him for good.

The departure of females had become a pattern in Seth's life.

He was done with relationships.

This evening, he had to remember to be very careful when he talked to Amy Ross. There were important things about Rachel Tyler that he needed to know—an awkward mystery that he needed to clarify—but he couldn't allow himself to be sidetracked by any further discussion of Amy's life as a single mother. If she'd been abandoned by a gold-plated jerk and left to struggle with a baby on her own, Seth didn't want to know about it.

He didn't want to feel pity for her and her daughter. And he didn't want to feel concern. Or longing.

He simply needed to get to the truth.

When Amy heard the soft tap on her door she felt a hot rush of adrenaline. Anxiously, she snatched a glance at her reflection and hoped she'd achieved a small improvement by changing into a fresh T-shirt and jeans.

Her hand was pleasingly steady as she reached for the door knob, but as soon as she saw Seth, tall and dark and filling her doorway, her steadiness deserted her.

She stepped outside quickly, and through the open doorway he sent a silent glance to the bed where Bella slept.

'Yes, she's out to it,' Amy said quietly and she let out a huff of breath, hoping it would settle her nerves.

'Would you like coffee?' he asked. 'Or something stronger?'

'Not especially,' she said, wanting a clear head, although she suspected she would benefit from a stiff drink right now.

He gave a curt nod towards the back veranda. 'Perhaps we should go out there, if it's not too wet. We shouldn't disturb Bella, but you'll still be able to hear her if she cries.'

'All right.'

Leaving a single bed lamp on, she closed the

door softly and followed him, and she felt nervous, as if she were going to a job interview she hadn't prepared for.

On the veranda, a wall light cast a soft glow over a trio of potted plants and two deeply cushioned cane chairs beside a wicker table.

Amy took a seat and she peered out at the curtain of rain, which was falling more softly now. She wondered what Seth wanted to 'chat' about. Avoiding that thought, she asked, 'How long will this rain last?'

'Hard to say.' He shrugged. 'In some wet seasons it rains non-stop for weeks.'

'That sounds depressing.'

'It can be. Most of us try to get away for at least part of the wet.'

'I've read about roads being cut off by floods.'

'That's why I have a plane,' Seth said in a dry, matter-of-fact tone.

A plane? Before Amy could register her astonishment, he said, 'So you've never been in the tropics before?'

'No, never.'

'You're not seeing it at its best. You should have come in winter.'

'But that would have been too late to help Rachel's book launch.'

'Ah, yes.' Seth looked out to the black and silent night, with only his profile showing to Amy. 'I was hoping we could talk about Rachel's book.'

Goosebumps broke out on Amy's arms. At least Seth hadn't guessed about Bella, but she wasn't sure if she was relieved or alarmed. What else could she tell him about the book?

If he realised that she'd come all this way, and imposed on his hospitality, on the pretext of promoting a book she knew next to nothing about, he would be justified in thinking she was crazy, *and* bad mannered.

She studied the dark lines of his brow and his nose and the angular jut of his jaw, but they gave her no clue to his thoughts.

He spoke without looking at her. 'You said you were Rachel Tyler's best friend.'

'Yes, I did, because it's true.'

'You've known her since you were fifteen.'

'Yes.'

'You've gossiped together.'

'I wouldn't call it gossip.' Amy sounded more prudish than she'd meant to. 'But sure, we talked a lot.'

'And yet she never talked to you about her book?'

'Not in any kind of detail.' Amy watched a moth dance into the pool of light. 'I—I think Rachel was superstitious. The book was terribly important to her, and I think she might have been afraid that it wouldn't be a success if she talked too much about it.'

'Did she tell you about her time at Serenity?'

'Very little,' Amy admitted with a sigh. Rachel had been totally absorbed by the aftermath of her trip north—her pregnancy and the birth of her baby.

'But she told you about me,' Seth said coldly. 'You knew how to find me.'

'Yes.'

Feeling hopelessly cornered, Amy closed her eyes. She hadn't wanted to tell Seth the whole story tonight. She'd wanted to wait till she'd been refreshed by a good night's sleep. She'd wanted to feel calm and composed, able to take her time and to choose her words carefully.

More importantly, she'd wanted to retain the upper hand in this, but Seth was pushing her, giving her no choice. She had to speak now. If he dragged the truth out of her, she would lose every ounce of credibility in his eyes.

And that mattered perhaps more than it should.

As she sat there, eyes closed, gathering courage, she heard the flutter of the moth's wings against the light globe and the sound of Seth's chair scraping on the wooden veranda boards. Her eyes flew open.

Seth was standing directly in front of her, towering over her. 'There's something you're not telling me, Amy.'

His voice was hard and as cutting as a sabre. He was trying to intimidate her, which was one thing Amy wouldn't tolerate. She'd learned in her own backyard to stand up to her brothers.

Bravely, she glared up at him. 'I don't like your tone.'

For a moment, he looked taken aback. 'I'm being very civil.'

He ran tense fingers through his hair, and time crawled as he stood there staring at her, while she stared back at him.

Eventually, his expression relaxed, and the next time he spoke his voice held no menace. 'Give me a break, Amy. I'm not used to playing these games. All I want is the truth. Why did you come here?'

'Because I need to talk to you.' Her eyes dropped to the moth, which now lay burned and dying on the bare floorboards. 'I have something very important to tell you.'

Even though Seth hadn't moved, she sensed the tension run through him, like a fault line in a wall of rock. She knew his mind was working at a million miles a minute and any second now he would put two and two together.

'If we're going to have this conversation, Seth, could you please sit down?'

He looked surprised, but to her relief he relented and resumed his seat, one long, jeans-clad leg crossed over the other, hands plunged deep in his pockets.

'I'm sorry,' he said. 'I didn't mean to upset you.'

'I'm sorry, too,' Amy admitted. 'I came here to do the right thing, but I've made rather a mess of it.'

Seth shot her a sharp glance, and she knew he was waiting for her to explain.

So this was it. The moment she'd feared.

'I'm not Bella's mother,' she said.

It was ages before he spoke, and in the stillness the rain continued to fall, needle-fine and shiny and silent.

'Is she Rachel's child?' he asked at last.

'Yes.'

*Yes...*

The word hung in the air, quivering like the vibrations of a tuning fork.

Amy wished she could feel relieved now that it was out, but she was too shocked by Seth's reaction.

Even in the subdued light, she could see the colour drain from his face. Then, silently, he slumped forward, elbows propped on his knees as he covered his face with his hands.

Shocked, she sat completely still, two fingers pressed against her lips, wishing she could recall the single word that had revealed so much.

Too much?

*Yes.* One little syllable had told him everything. There was no need to add that Bella was his daughter.

The fact that Amy had brought Bella all this way pointed to it, and a few simple calculations confirmed the facts. Seth only had to count back to know that Bella's conception had occurred during the time Rachel had spent at Serenity.

With him.

And, clearly, it was the worst possible news.

A cool breeze whipped onto the veranda, spraying fine rain over them.

Amy shivered and rubbed at her arms. 'Seth,' she said gently. 'I'm sorry. I know this is a shock.'

He didn't respond at first, then slowly he lowered his hands and let them hang loosely between his knees. He didn't look at her and he didn't speak, but Amy saw the movement of his throat as he swallowed.

'I came here, because I—I thought you should know,' she said. 'I thought it was important. Not because I want money from you, but because—well, because Bella's such a sweetheart.'

The thin, cold pricks of rain continued as she waited for a response from him. When it didn't come, she went on, desperate now to make her point. 'I think Bella's the cutest thing on two legs, you see. And, to me, it seemed unfair that you didn't know about her.'

At last Seth turned to her and she was shocked by the banked despair she saw in his eyes and in the deep lines that bracketed his mouth.

His eyes were bleak, but to her surprise he almost smiled. 'Don't feel bad. You've done the right thing.'

It was reassuring to hear this, but she wished he looked happier.

'I'm not planning to offload Bella,' she felt compelled to explain. 'You don't have to worry about that, Seth. I'm totally prepared to keep her with me and to take care of her.'

'I'm sure that's best,' he said quietly.

She let out her breath on a sigh. This was awful, so different from how she'd imagined everything before she'd set out on this journey. She'd anticipated the possibility of fierce anger, or disdainful disbelief. She'd been worried that Seth might try to take Bella away from her, but the last thing she'd expected was this shocked and horrified acceptance.

When his gaze met hers again, his eyes warmed just a little. 'So what's your relationship to Bella? Are you her guardian?'

Amy nodded. 'Rachel had no other family.'

'Really? No one at all?'

Amy was surprised he knew so little. 'She was an only child,' she told him. 'Her father has passed away, and her mother's in an aged care facility, and she's not at all well. Her parents were in their fifties when she was born. Apparently, they'd never expected to have a child, and Rachel was a huge surprise.'

After a bit, he said quietly, 'That might explain why Rachel was…*different*.'

'She *was* different, wasn't she?' Amy's mouth twisted in a wistful smile as she remembered her friend. 'She was brilliant, a ton of fun, but—yes—different.'

Seth nodded and looked away quickly, and she wondered if he'd been deeply in love with Rachel. The thought caused an unhappy pang.

'You're doing a great job with Bella,' he said.

'It's no hardship. I love her.'

His piercing blue gaze swung back to study her for a heart-stopping stretch of time, and then he rose abruptly.

'Thank you,' he said simply, and she knew their conversation was over.

They went back inside the house and Amy shivered as breeze from a ceiling fan chilled her damp skin. She felt miserable as she stood outside her bedroom door.

'Goodnight,' Seth said. 'I hope you'll be comfortable.'

'I'm sure I will.' Then she remembered. 'Just

a minute, Seth. I have something you might like to see.' She went into the room and fetched a photo album that she'd brought with her, especially for him. As she gave it to him his hands brushed hers and her breath caught as she felt the heat of his skin.

'Thanks,' he murmured, gripping the album tightly.

The house was silent, listening.

He seemed to remember his manners as a host. 'Are you sure you wouldn't like something to drink before you turn in?'

'Could I make myself a cup of tea?'

'I can get it for you.'

'No, it's OK, honestly. I can find my way around the kitchen.'

'Be my guest,' he said, gesturing down the hallway to the kitchen, and with a curt nod he left her.

Amy's sense of anticlimax was overwhelming, and a warm shower and a brisk rub down with a luxuriously thick bath towel didn't help her to feel any better. Standing in her nightgown between the twin beds, she looked down at Bella, sound asleep and blameless, hugging her plush pink pig, her mouth slightly ajar as she slept.

She felt an urge to climb into the bed and to cuddle the little girl close, seeking comfort and reassurance from her small, warm weight in her arms.

*Have I done the right thing, baby?*

She padded on bare feet down the darkened hall to the kitchen and found an electric jug and the makings for tea. On her way back, mug in hand, she saw light coming from beneath a door just across the hallway.

Was it Seth's room?

The possibility made her skin flush hot.

*Fool.*

In her room, she piled up her pillows and sat in bed in a small pool of lamplight, nursing a mug of hot, sweet tea.

She thought about Rachel, and was swamped by a tidal wave of grief. If only she hadn't invited Rachel to the launch party. For the trillionth time, she wished that she could go back into the past and change that night. Rachel had always been so full of life, so brimming with can-do confidence and charisma. She shouldn't be dead.

Their friendship had been so strong, an attraction of opposites. Rachel was brilliant and wild and she'd always claimed that Amy was calming and steadying.

'Amy's my anchor,' she used to tell people.

Guys were forever falling in love with Rachel—so much so that she should have had a warning light, like a lighthouse. Amy's brother, Ryan, had been smitten, but he'd come to his senses eventually and married his sensible, sweet Jane instead.

For her part, Rachel had loved the attention of men, always had a boyfriend on tap, but somehow she'd managed to stay immune, never really falling in love.

Until her trip north.

'You should have been there, Ames,' she'd said, on that night she'd finally opened up. 'I needed you there, to keep me on the ground. I lost my head completely.'

Swiping at tears, Amy thought about Seth. She wondered if he was looking at the photo album now. Would he sleep tonight? Or was he totally calm again?

Was he thinking about Rachel? About Bella?

He'd looked so terrible tonight when she'd told him her news, and the memory of the deep lines of pain etched in his face sent a throbbing ache to the middle of her chest.

It was so silly to care so much about a man she'd only just met, but she couldn't help it. There was something about Seth Reardon that *got* to her—something elemental and deep. Whether he was happy or sad, whenever she was near him, she felt in danger of drowning.

She'd known, from the moment she first saw him—gosh, had it only been this morning?—that he wasn't a man who would take fatherhood lightly. Chances were, Seth wouldn't take any relationship lightly—which meant there was a distinct possibility that he'd really, *really* loved Rachel.

Without warning, Amy's tears began to fall in

earnest, and she buried her face in the pillow so she wouldn't wake Bella.

The photo album lay abandoned on the nightstand.

Seth had taken a look at it, leafing quickly through the pages, catching glimpses of Bella as a tiny newborn, and later, as a gummy, smiling infant…later still, as a sturdy toddler, learning to walk…

He'd seen pictures of Rachel looking surprisingly maternal, and healthy and happy. There'd even been a shot of Amy, hovering somewhere in the background behind a cake with pink icing and two striped candles. But he'd had to set the book aside. It was too hard to look at these happy snaps.

Amy had offered them to him in all innocence, but she had no idea of the size and force of the bombshell she'd dropped this evening.

She thought he'd fathered Rachel Tyler's baby. He'd never dreamed that Rachel was pregnant when she left Serenity, but, hell, in many ways everything would be a whole lot easier if he were the little girl's father. He would face up to the responsibility, and he could have worked something out with Amy—a way to share custody of Bella, perhaps. Truth be told, the thought of spending more time with Amy was enticing.

But it was a fantasy.

He wasn't Bella's father. He hadn't slept with Rachel.

Not once.

Never.

The real story was something else entirely, and it smothered him with a mountain of guilt and heartache.

While Rachel had flirted openly with him almost as soon as she'd arrived at Serenity, Seth had sensed she could spell trouble and he'd given her the brush-off, so she'd set her sights…elsewhere…

With tragic consequences.

Those consequences were the cross Seth had to bear, but they were too painful to share this evening with a warm-hearted, soft-eyed girl like Amy.

With a harsh groan, he launched to his feet and began to prowl.

This whole business was more complicated than Amy could possibly have imagined and he needed time—days, weeks, *years*—to work out the best way to explain it to her.

Damn it, he didn't want to burden her with the truth. Not so soon. She'd been such a loyal friend to Rachel. She'd put her career on hold and she'd devoted herself to Bella, and she'd come all this way, to do something Rachel should have done three years ago.

Reaching for the album, Seth looked again at the photo of Amy, smiling in the background. Her dark eyes were so warm and pretty, and just looking at her made him want to smile.

She was as generous and open-hearted as his uncle had been when he'd taken Seth in after his father died, giving him a home, an education, a sense of belonging. Family.

Seth owed so much to his father's younger and much admired brother, after whom he'd been named.

But now…damn it…what was the right thing to do?

He couldn't turn his back on this little girl. How had Amy described her? *Cutest thing on two legs.*

Too true.

Thing was, it would be easy to wash his hands of this, to tell Amy she was mistaken, that he wasn't the father. Send her packing.

Except—he felt such a weight of responsibility…and it was all so painful…and even though Amy was warm and compassionate, he didn't feel ready to talk to a woman he'd just met about what had happened…

He needed time.

'Wake up, Amy! Wake up!'

Amy felt small fingers trying to prise her eyelids apart.

'It's too early,' she moaned, refusing to open her eyes.

She'd had a dreadful night, endlessly tossing and turning, and she felt as if she'd fallen into a deep sleep only five minutes ago. But a sudden knock at the door brought her smartly awake.

'Man!' Bella squealed, gleefully slipping from the bed. 'Man at the door!'

With a groan, Amy pushed her bedclothes aside and swung her feet to the floor. She had no idea of the time, but daylight was streaming through the shutters.

Bella was banging on the door. 'Hello, man!'

'His name's Seth,' Amy grumbled. She couldn't remember where she'd left her dressing gown and she grabbed up a silk wrap to throw around her shoulders to cover her nightgown. 'Bella, you can't keep calling him man. Say Seth.'

'Sef.'

'That's better.' Amy grimaced at her reflection. She looked a fright—hair everywhere, dark circles under her eyes.

There was another knock.

'Hello, Sef man,' Bella called through the door.

With one hand clasping the wrap modestly over her front, Amy ran frantic fingers through her hair, but she knew it wouldn't improve her appearance. She opened the door.

Seth, freshly showered and shaved, was rather

too much at such an early hour, but she didn't have time to go weak at the knees. She was distracted by Bella's shriek of joy.

'Hello, Sef!' the little girl shouted, and she beamed a gorgeous smile up at him, holding her arms up to be lifted.

For a moment, Amy thought he might resist the appeal of those little outstretched hands, but after only the briefest hesitation he bent down and scooped Bella high.

'How are you this morning, possum?'

Giggling, Bella planted a wet kiss on his cheek and hugged him hard. Amy choked back her surprise. When had this pair become such firm friends?

She watched Seth's ears redden, but with the typical fickleness of a two-year-old the little girl was soon wriggling to be set down again.

Seth's smile was shy as he took in Amy's dishevelled appearance. 'I see I'm too early for you.'

'I forgot you cattlemen get up at the crack of dawn.'

His eyes shimmered with mild amusement as

he took in her nightgown and her efforts at modesty. He glanced at his wristwatch.

'What's the time?' she asked.

'Seven-forty.'

'Oh…well…not exactly dawn, then.'

'Breakfast's at eight. Is that too early?'

'No, that's fine, thank you.'

She dropped her gaze, unsure what to say now. She wondered if Seth had adjusted to the news that he was Bella's father. Even though he looked calm enough, he could be angry that she'd come to Serenity under false pretences. Last night she'd lain awake worrying and imagining that he'd send her packing this morning, straight after breakfast.

'It's stopped raining,' Seth said. 'So you might have an opportunity to take some photos after all.'

'Really? That's great.' She felt her heart skip in relief. So, not straight after breakfast, at least.

Behind her, Bella began bouncing on her bed, treating it like a trampoline.

Amy whirled around. 'Bella, stop that, or you'll fall.' She reached out to catch the little girl's hand.

'I was thinking it would be good if you could stay on for a bit longer than we'd planned,' Seth said, ignoring the distraction.

Amy blinked at him from beneath tumbled hair.

'You came here because you wanted me to get to know Bella,' he said. 'So it doesn't really make sense that you should rush away too soon.'

'I—I—' Catching giggling Bella in mid-jump, Amy held her close to keep her still. 'I'd have to change my flights.'

'I'm sure we could arrange that.'

She rubbed at her forehead, trying to clear her sleep-fuzzed brain. 'You were so upset last night. Are you sure you want us to stay?'

'I've had time to think, to get used to everything. I'd like the chance to get to know Bella. I'd like her—both of you—to enjoy Serenity.'

'Will your uncle mind?'

Seth's face seemed to cave in. Shadows darkened his eyes and his throat worked. 'My uncle's not here. He died a couple of years ago.'

'Oh, I'm sorry,' she said, but it was hard to feel the appropriate depth of sympathy when she hadn't known his uncle, especially when her stomach was fluttering madly at the possibility of staying on, alone with Seth.

Amy couldn't think why she was hesitating. This invitation was exactly what she'd come north to achieve. Twenty-four hours ago, time on Serenity so that Bella could get to know her father had been her primary goal. Her dream.

Twenty-four hours ago, she hadn't met Seth Reardon. She hadn't developed a silly, useless and problematic crush that would only get worse if she spent more time with him. But there were other problems, too. There was every chance that Seth would fall for sweet Bella as swiftly and certainly as she had fallen. How would she cope if Seth wanted to keep Bella?

Part of Amy wanted very much to whisk the little girl safely back to Melbourne and to resume her life. She couldn't give her little girl up.

She would have to make it clear that Bella couldn't stay at Serenity permanently. That had never been her plan.

Amy knew how Rachel had felt about remote

Cape York, and yesterday she'd seen for herself how far Seth's home was from anywhere else. It was no place for a single dad to try to raise a sociable toddler.

'Look, I'll give you time to think about it,' Seth said, backing down the hall. 'We can talk about it at breakfast.'

'No, it's OK.' Amy sent him an apologetic smile. 'It's a good idea and we'd love to stay. Thank you.'

'Terrific.' Seth smiled in a way that put creases in the suntanned skin around his bright blue eyes. 'We'll have breakfast on the front veranda at a little after eight. You just have to turn left at the end of the hallway.'

'OK. Thanks.'

It was only after Seth had gone that Amy realised her wrap had fallen during their conversation—while she was trying to catch the bouncing Bella, no doubt. She'd been standing here, talking to Seth in her fine cotton nightgown, exposed in all its transparent glory.

A glance in the mirror showed her just how

much of her Seth had seen, and a blushing river of heat flooded her.

At least he'd been too polite to stare at her breasts.

She wished she could take more comfort from that.

# CHAPTER FOUR

HOLDING Bella's hand, Amy went down the hallway, turned left, as Seth had directed, and walked into a stream of sunshine.

And an idyllic tropical paradise.

'Goodness, Bella, where are we?'

Last night, entering by the back steps in the rainy dark, Amy had realised that Seth's home was comfortable—but now she saw that not one thing about it came even close to her idea of a cattleman's residence.

The veranda at the front of the house was so deep it formed large, outdoor rooms. She paused in the doorway to take it all in.

From here she could see a dining area and, beyond that, bamboo cane lounge chairs grouped around a coffee table, and, beyond that again, a desk with a telephone and a high-backed chair. Gently circling ceiling fans and huge potted palms gave the whole area an elegant, Oriental air.

She saw the garden beyond the veranda and gasped… Instead of hectares of dry, grassy paddocks, the Serenity homestead was fronted by terraces of smooth lawns and lush tropical gardens where delicate orchids grew side by side with bright bougainvillea and graceful palms. Heavens, there was even a swimming pool on one of the terraces.

The entire grounds were set in a haven of green on a densely wooded hillside, with views to white sandy beaches, a bright, glittering sea, and the dark emerald silhouettes of offshore islands.

It was gorgeous. Unreal. Amy felt as if she'd woken up at a resort and, at any minute, a waiter would appear to offer her a long, colourful drink with clinking ice cubes and a tiny paper umbrella.

Seth rose from the dining table and came towards them, smiling at the stunned expression on Amy's face.

'This is amazing,' she said.

'Glad you like it.'

'But—' She made a sweeping gesture that took in the gardens edged by rainforest and the view. 'Where are your cattle?'

Seth laughed. 'We passed through the grazing country yesterday. Over to the west. Not far away at all. There's only a narrow fringe of this rainforest along the coastal mountains.'

'But it's beautiful.' She could so easily imagine Rachel living here, soaking up the exotic atmosphere.

That thought brought Amy straight back to earth.

Which was just as well. She knew she couldn't allow herself to be carried away by the beauty of Seth's home.

It would be prudent to keep Rachel at the forefront of her thoughts. She had to remember that it was right here, in this setting, that Rachel and Seth had been swept away by a passionate liaison.

Bella was tugging at her hand. 'Look, look! A swimming pool!' She tried to pull Amy towards the sparkling blue water. 'My go swimming.'

'Not now,' Amy told her. 'We're going to have breakfast.'

Bending quickly, she picked the little girl up and hugged her, and as they took their places at the dining table she wished she didn't feel so unaccountably afraid.

Her desire for Bella to know her father had been driven purely by emotion. Families were important to Amy. Her own family was big and noisy and loving and she hated that Bella knew no one who was related to her by blood. Now, suddenly, Amy was looking at this gorgeous property, and was forced to accept practical realities that outweighed emotion.

Seth Reardon was seriously wealthy. He didn't merely own vast tracts of land and mobs of valuable cattle. His home was beautiful and comfortable and he had domestic help, and an aeroplane, for heaven's sake.

Bella was his daughter, his potential heiress, and if Seth wanted to he could hire a nanny for her and she could live here with him quite happily and safely.

Last night, when he'd been stunned and shocked, Seth had agreed that Amy could take Bella back to Melbourne. Naively, she'd had no doubt that she was the very best person to raise the little girl. She'd even broken up with Dominic because she believed that so vehemently.

But already, less than a day after arriving at Serenity, she was having deep misgivings about her right to make such demands.

Had Rachel felt similar doubts? Was that why she'd kept her pregnancy secret?

'Let's eat,' Seth said, watching her with a puzzled smile, and she turned her attention to the food.

Clearly Ming was a genius, and their breakfast was a meal of stunning simplicity. A beautiful fruit platter of passionfruit, vividly hued pawpaw and mango, and a star-shaped fruit Amy had never seen before, was followed by perfectly delicious, lightly spiced mushrooms and tomatoes on toasted home-made bread.

Bella ate a banana cut up in a bowl of yoghurt with golden circles of honey drizzled on top.

'That's one of her favourite breakfasts,' Amy

told Seth as she watched the little girl eagerly wielding her spoon.

'I took a guess when I suggested fruit and yoghurt to Ming. He's not used to cooking for a two-year-old.'

'Are you?' she couldn't help asking. 'Have you had much experience with children?'

'Only what I've observed with other people's kids.'

Which meant he was more observant than most bachelors, she decided unhappily. Again, she felt an anxious swoop in her chest at the possibility of giving up Bella.

'I'm guessing that Bella might enjoy a play in the pool before it gets too hot,' Seth said when they'd finished their meal.

'I'm sure she would. She loves the water.' Amy was grateful that she'd included their bathers when she'd packed, but she'd expected to be swimming in an Outback creek or a river, not a beautifully tiled, sparkling, manmade pool.

'Go swimming,' Bella announced, pulling at Amy's hand.

Amy gave her a wistful smile. 'When your breakfast's gone down.'

But it wasn't very long before she gave in and Bella was racing ahead of her down the smooth stone steps to greet Seth at the edge of the pool.

'Look, Sef!' the little girl announced with great excitement. 'I'm a ballerdina!' She spun around, so he could admire her red and white spotted swimsuit edged with cute frills.

'You're a beautiful ballerina,' he assured her. 'Bella the water-baby ballerina.'

His smiling gaze flickered to Amy and she was glad she'd splurged on a new swimsuit for herself. She knew she was no real beauty, but she'd always been told she had decent legs, and the swimsuit was dark green and perfectly cut to flatter her figure. Even though she wasn't trying to impress this man, she was quietly pleased that she looked OK.

Seth looked more than OK, of course, in black swimming trunks and with a towel slung around his magnificent shoulders.

It was hard to stop stealing glances at his bare chest and his deeply bronzed, fabulous physique.

'Well, let's have a splash, shall we, Bella?'

The little girl loved the water, but she couldn't swim, so she needed constant help and supervision and Amy was grateful that she was kept busy. It helped to ignore Seth while he swam up and down the pool with smooth, powerful strokes.

After a bit, he joined them. 'Your turn,' he told Amy, sending her a grin that made his teeth flash white against his tan. 'I'll look after Bella, while you have a swim.'

It was unsettling to hand Bella over, almost as if it was a foretaste of the future. Amy struggled with her reluctance. 'You need to watch her like a hawk,' she told Seth. 'She thinks she can swim.'

'I'll be careful.'

She had no choice but to trust him. 'She's not scared of the water, and she doesn't mind putting her face under.'

Bella was so excited and wet and wriggly that the handover was precarious. Amy almost dropped the little girl when she felt Seth's bare leg brush against hers and she fumbled again when their hands touched and they bumped elbows.

It was bittersweet relief to leave them at last and to swim away in a careful breaststroke to the deep end of the pool. As she swam she could hear Bella's delighted squeals and laughter.

When she reached the other end, she turned and looked back and saw them together—father and daughter, looking so alike with their dark wet hair, sleek against their skulls—and she felt another tremor of fear deep inside.

Was she being silly, or was she really in danger of losing Bella? Would Seth demand that his daughter live with him?

The thought brought a hot swirl of panic. She'd been so sure she was doing the right thing, that bringing Bella here was in line with Rachel's intentions.

But now she'd met Seth and seen his beautiful home she couldn't help wondering why Rachel had objected to living here. She wondered if there was a deeper reason behind Rachel's avoidance of this meeting with Seth. And was there also an equally good reason why she'd named Amy, and not Seth, as Bella's guardian?

Amy was sure she was entitled to the role. She adored Bella, had been involved in her life since her birth, had actually been present at her birth.

She would never forget that incredible, joyous morning. Now, the possibility that she might lose Bella made her want to weep.

She dived under the water to wash away the possibility of tears. She had to be strong, to remember that she'd come here for this—to allow Bella and her father to meet—and she was pleased they were getting on so well. He'd accepted that Amy was Bella's guardian and she had to have faith in her decisions and in her instincts that told her Seth Reardon could be trusted.

Even so, the few days that she would spend here suddenly felt like a dangerously long stretch of time.

'Everything's so different and exotic here,' Amy said later, waving her hand to the view of the terraced hillside and the bright blue sea framed by a tangle of rainforest jungle. 'I find it hard to believe that I'm still in Australia. I feel as if I've crossed hemispheres.'

'In a way you have.' Seth sent her a slow smile, aware that it was becoming a habit, this smiling at Amy. It was highly likely that, between them, she and Bella had made him smile more times in the past twenty-four hours than he had in the past twelve months.

He said, 'Weren't you telling me yesterday that Serenity is as far from Melbourne as London is from Moscow?'

She turned to him, giving him the full benefit of her warm chocolate eyes, and he was very glad he'd suggested that they take this time to sit on the veranda, drinking coffee after lunch, while Bella napped.

'It must have been quite a culture shock for you to move all the way from Sydney to here,' she said earnestly. 'You were only twelve. That's smack on the edge of adolescence, when everything looms larger than life.'

'Actually, I think the fact that everything was so different here helped me,' he said. 'I was overawed by this place, but I thought it was incredibly exciting, and my uncle kept me busy from first thing in the morning till I fell into bed at night. He turned my life into an adventure. I'm sure I'd have found it much harder to get over my father's death if I'd stayed in Sydney.'

Surprised that he'd told Amy so much, he reached for his coffee cup and drank deeply.

Her face was soft with sympathy, as if she was picturing how it had been for him. 'It can't have been easy though, when you didn't have a mother.'

From force of habit, Seth brushed her comment aside. He had no intention of explaining about his mother. She was a subject he never talked about. There was no reason to discuss her.

But Amy had hooked her elbow over the arm of her chair and she was leaning towards him, watching him with her complete attention. Two small lines of worry drew her brows low and her brown eyes were rounded with concern, her pink lips parted. Seth found himself wanting to lean closer, too, to kiss those soft, inviting lips, to kiss away that frown.

It would be so easy.

So incredibly satisfying.

And…totally inappropriate. She hadn't come here for a fling.

All day he'd been struggling to blank out the picture of Amy this morning in her flimsy cotton nightdress. He tried not to think about the soft round outline of her breasts, the smooth skin of her shoulders, the tapering curve of her waist.

But Amy was different from Rachel. Seth knew she hadn't been planning seduction, and he could have sworn that she hadn't even noticed when her wrap slipped from her shoulders.

There'd been no flirting in the pool today either. But, heaven help him, he could still see the back view of her as she climbed the pool ladder. World-class legs. Lovely behind. Movements so graceful and feminine he couldn't help but stare.

*Damn it*, the very fact that Amy's sexiness was unintentional, and the knowledge that she wasn't trying to seduce him, made his desire for her all the stronger.

But he shouldn't have been checking her out. Just as he shouldn't be thinking about kissing her now.

He couldn't afford to start an affair with little Bella's guardian when he knew that it could never go anywhere. The child needed stability in her life, and he'd learned the hard way that women and his lifestyle didn't mix. For the past few years, he'd worked hard at keeping his distance from women like Amy—intelligent, warm-hearted, home-and-hearth-loving women.

The marrying kind.

Even so, he knew it would only take the first taste of her tender mouth, the first touch of his lips to her soft, warm skin and he'd be craving more.

He drew in a sharp breath.

*Don't even think about it.*

Why was it so hard to remember his past mistakes?

*For pity's sake, man, just answer the woman's question.*

He said, 'My mother left after my father died.'

'Left?' Shock made Amy's voice tremble. 'Are you saying she left *you*?'

Seth shrugged and forced a smile. 'Ever since I can remember, she'd had her sights set on Hollywood, and without my father to hold her back she was free to go.'

'But she wasn't free, Seth. She had you.' Amy stared at him, with a hand pressed to her throat. Her dark eyes were clouded, as if he'd told her something completely beyond her comprehension. 'You'd just lost your father. You were only twelve. Why couldn't she keep you with her?'

It was a question that had eaten at Seth for years. Even now, he could feel the agonising slug of loss that had flattened him, when he'd finally understood what his mother's choice had meant.

Her longing for fame and glamour had outweighed her sense of responsibility.

Bottom line, she hadn't loved him enough.

Regretting that he'd started this line of talk, he sent Amy another shrugging smile. 'I was better off up here with my uncle.'

'I can't believe that.'

'I didn't believe it at first, but with the benefit of hindsight I know it was best.'

Amy looked as if she couldn't possibly agree.

'Think about it,' Seth told her. 'What twelve-year-old boy would choose to live in a low-rent flat in a huge metropolis like Los Angeles, when he could be here, learning to ride horses, to raise cattle, to fish and to skin-dive, to explore deserted islands, and to paddle a kayak?'

'I guess,' she said uncertainly.

'I owe my uncle a great deal.'

As if she needed time to think about this, she picked up the coffee pot. 'Would you like a refill?'

'Thanks.' He held out his cup and he admired the unconscious elegance of her slim wrists and hands as she lifted the teapot and poured.

She was dressed for the tropical heat in a soft blue cotton dress, with loose sleeves that left her smooth, lightly tanned arms free. Her hair, which had dried in natural waves after their swim, was twisted into a loose knot from which wispy curls strayed.

Her citified neatness was beginning to unravel and Seth found the process utterly fascinating. He wasn't sure which version of Amy he preferred, but one thing was certain—he was finding it close to impossible to remain detached, an aloof observer.

But he had to keep his distance. In a matter of days she was returning to Melbourne. She was a city girl. End of story.

Amy filled her cup and added milk, then settled down to resume their conversation. 'So did your mother make it big in Hollywood?'

'She's had walk-on parts in daytime soap operas, but that's about it.'

'Has she made enough money to live on?'

'I have no idea, but it doesn't really matter. She remarried,' Seth said coldly. 'Found herself a cashed-up Californian.'

'Has she ever been here?'

'Once, when she dropped me off,' he said, unhappily aware that he'd revealed much more than he'd intended. It was time to put a stop to these personal questions. Years ago, he'd learned to live without his mother and he wasn't going to admit to a tender-hearted woman like Amy Ross that his only contact with her had been letters on his eighteenth and twenty-first birthdays with generous cheques attached.

He drained his coffee cup and stood. 'I'm afraid I have business to attend to and I'm sure you'd appreciate time to yourself while Bella's asleep.'

'I'd like to take photographs of your grounds, if that's all right.'

'Be my guest. But keep to the open areas. Don't go wandering off into the rainforest, or down the track to the beach.'

Amy frowned. 'Do you think I'll get lost?'

'I'm assuming you'd rather not come face to face with an amethystine python, or a salt-water crocodile.'

The colour drained from her face and he winced. In one breath he'd completely ruined her stay.

'I'm exaggerating the danger,' he said more gently. 'People have been living here for decades quite safely. But I'd rather you didn't go exploring without me.'

'Yes,' she acceded, still looking pale. 'That might be best.'

'So promise me for now that you won't go beyond the garden.'

Amy gave him her word.

# CHAPTER FIVE

As SHE watched Seth stride away, Amy almost changed her mind about setting foot outside the house. The spectre of snakes and crocodiles scared her to death and in a panicky rush she ran back to the bedroom to make sure that Bella was still sleeping safely.

The windows and doors to their room were screened, however, and no creepy-crawlies could find their way in, thank God. Bella was fine.

She knew Seth's claim was true—plenty of people had lived here and avoided being eaten. Rachel had stayed here for six weeks and she'd never mentioned any special dangers. Then again, Rachel had kept quiet about a lot of things in the north.

Including Seth.

But Amy had already tortured herself enough over that man. All morning, she'd driven herself crazy fretting over his relationship with Rachel, his plans for Bella, and her own giddy pulse rate whenever he was near.

Taking several deep breaths, she swore to put him out of her mind, and she set off, camera in hand, to explore his garden.

Which was lovely. Really lovely.

Again she wondered why Rachel had never mentioned how gorgeous this place was. She'd made so few comments, hadn't shown any pictures. Nothing. Had she saved it all for her book?

Amy didn't know the names of many of the tropical plants, but as she walked she recognised hibiscus, orchids and bougainvilleas growing lushly amidst ferns and palms. She loved the showiness and variety of the lavishly hued tropical flowers and leaves.

The butterflies and birds were extra bright and beautiful, too. All living things here were wonderfully vivid. Nature at double strength. As she walked down twisting paths, she felt as if her senses were zapped onto high alert.

She was surrounded by fragrances—the scents of frangipani, of ginger and cardamom, mixed with a pervading smell of damp earth and vegetation. There was a constant peep-peep-peeping sound, which, Seth had already explained, came from tiny tree frogs in the nearby forest.

Here in the tropics there was a sense of life teeming and lush, pushing to the max, and she was aware of an indefinable something that stirred her, a constant pulse-raising excitement and restlessness.

Perhaps that was why her thoughts zeroed straight back to Seth.

She couldn't help it. He was such a fascinating puzzle.

He'd said he was fine about his mother's defection, but Amy had been watching him closely, and despite his brave words she'd seen dark pain in his eyes and in the tightening set of his mouth.

Her heart ached for him, but his brave stoicism also frightened her. How could they come to an agreement about Bella's future when his attitude to mothers and motherhood was almost the polar opposite of hers?

Amy adored her mum and she adored caring for Bella, but if Seth had managed so famously in this remote place without any contact with his mother, he might easily assume that Bella would be fine here, too.

And where, Amy wondered, did that leave her?

It was a relief, on rounding a tall clump of pink ginger, to be distracted by an elderly man wearing a wide-brimmed hat of woven cane and happily hacking at palm fronds with a long-handled machete.

'Hi,' Amy called, waving to catch his attention.

In no time, she'd introduced herself and learned that he was Hans, who'd grown up in Indonesia, and had worked as a gardener on Serenity for more than twenty years.

'Can I show you my garden?' he asked in response to her eager compliments, and when she assured him she'd love that he grinned so widely his face disappeared into a mass of brown wrinkles.

For the next half-hour, Amy was highly entertained *and* educated, and she tried, once again, to put Seth Reardon and his potential threats to her happiness firmly out of her mind.

Seth didn't return to the homestead until it was close to dusk. By then, the sky had turned smoky aqua and pink and the garden was filled with purple shadows. Amy was about to take Bella inside for her bath when she saw Seth coming across the lawn to the house.

There was something tired about his shoulders that she hadn't noticed before, but his smile was bright when Bella ran to greet him with her usual bouncing enthusiasm.

He scooped her up in his arms and swung her so high that the little girl squealed, then begged for more.

Seth laughed. 'That's enough for now.' He shot Amy a bright-eyed glance. 'Come with me and I'll show you magic fireflies.'

'Fireflies?' Amy and Bella chorused together.

He nodded towards the darkening forest. 'Over here. Come on, I'll show you.'

They went down a flight of stone steps to a lower terrace, crossed the lawn to a dark line of trees, and Amy saw a narrow track leading away into the shadowy depths of the forest. Seth, who was holding Bella with one arm, suddenly reached for Amy's hand.

Heat raced over her skin like a fire out of control.

'Stay with me,' he said quietly and for a giddy, heart-stumbling moment, she fancied he was asking her to…stay here…

To live with him at Serenity.

And then, crazily, even though she'd only known him for two days, she felt an astonishing impulse to say yes.

'We'll take this track slowly,' he said.

*Oh, good grief.*

Embarrassment flooded Amy as she realised her mistake. Seth wanted her to stay close to him on the darkened track. Of course he wasn't talking about a romantic future.

Of course, of course.

Silently, she cursed her ridiculous reaction. For heaven's sake. Her job was to protect Bella's future happiness, and she had to remember that Seth might yet make unreasonable demands and become their enemy.

'W-what about the s-n-a-k-e-s?' she whispered, spelling out the word so she didn't frighten Bella.

'You'll be OK with me. I know what to look for.'

'Are you sure?'

She saw the flash of his teeth as he grinned at her. 'Tree snakes aren't really dangerous, unless you're a bird or a little possum.'

Her heart was thundering like a Mack truck, but the problem wasn't so much her fear of snakes as the intimate warmth of Seth's hand enclosing hers. She registered every detail—the slightly rough texture of his palm, the individual pressure of each of his fingers.

Seth took them deeper into the forest, dodging hanging vines and buttressed tree roots. The frogs were silent now and the trees crowded close, but just when Amy wondered if they were mad to continue into the gathering gloom they reached a clearing—and Seth released her hand.

The sudden feeling of loss was alarming, but Amy was soon gasping with amazement as tiny pinpricks of light flitted and danced in the dusky glade. The fireflies flashed in front of them, behind them, and above them, and they looked exactly like tiny glowing fairies.

Seth was right—they were magic. Truly magic and utterly entrancing.

'They're so beautiful,' Amy said softly. 'Look Bella, see the fireflies. They're like fairies.'

'Fairies,' Bella repeated in hushed awe.

'Aren't they pretty?'

The little girl nodded, and for once she was too entranced to speak. She simply wound her arms around Seth's neck and hugged him more tightly, and he smiled and kissed her cheek.

'Is that firefly all right? It doesn't seem able to fly,' Amy said, pointing to a blinking light that had stayed on the ground the whole time.

Seth laughed softly. 'That's a female. She stays down there quietly, waiting till a flashing male appeals to her, and then she flashes back, signalling her interest.'

'Oh.' Amy wished she hadn't asked and she was sure she was still blushing when it was time to head back.

'I didn't bring a torch,' Seth told her. 'So you need to stay close.'

He took her hand again and she vowed to remain calm and sensible as they made their way back.

Conversation would be a helpful distraction, she decided, so she told Seth that she'd made friends with Hans, the gardener, and that she'd visited the kitchen to talk to Ming. Bella chattered about fairies, then promptly begged for another swim.

'Not till tomorrow,' Seth told her gently but firmly, as if he was already completely comfortable with his new role as her father.

Amy half expected Bella to ask again for a swim, pleading and putting on her whiny voice, but the little girl accepted Seth's ruling without a murmur.

They reached the edge of the trees where they could see the lights from the house spilling across the terraced lawns, and just when Amy expected Seth to release her she felt his thumb stroke the back of her hand. Slowly. Deliberately.

Just once.

A trembling thrill raced from her breastbone to her toes.

She knew it hadn't been an accident.

She couldn't breathe, but then Seth released her hand and he set Bella down to run ahead of them over the smooth lawn.

Still trembling from his touch, Amy sent a quick glance in his direction, but his attention was focused entirely on Bella, and he was smiling as he watched her skipping and flapping her arms in the warm night air.

'She's trying to be a firefly,' he said.

'She's having a great time here,' Amy admitted softly.

'She is, isn't she?' He was still smiling.

She wanted to remind him of his intention to let Bella return to Melbourne at the end of their stay, but she was silenced by the shining light in his eyes. For the first time since she'd met him, he looked genuinely happy.

After Seth showered and changed into fresh clothes, he went through to the kitchen, where he found Bella at the kitchen table, glowing pink and clean after her bath, smelling of baby talcum powder and wolfing down a bowl of Ming's special chicken congee.

'Hi, Sef,' Bella called, waving her spoon at him. 'My eating dinner.'

'Lucky you.' He found himself smiling back at her. He'd been smiling so much lately it was a wonder his face hadn't cracked. 'Is Amy about?' he asked Ming.

'She's taking a shower.' Ming turned from the stove, shot a shrewd glance Seth's way, and grinned. 'I reckon she's doing the same as you.'

'What's that?'

'Getting spruced up for your dinner date.'

'It isn't a date.'

Ming's keen gaze took in Seth's clean moleskin trousers and neatly pressed shirt and Seth felt the back of his neck grow hot.

'I thought I explained,' he said tightly. 'Amy's a friend of Rachel's. You remember Rachel? Rachel Tyler?'

'Of course.' The cook frowned and turned back

to the stove. 'But Amy Ross is nothing like Rachel.'

'No,' Seth agreed as he helped Bella to scrape the last of the chicken and rice porridge from the bottom of her bowl. 'Amy's not remotely like Rachel. They're chalk and cheese.'

He heard a sound behind him and turned to find Amy in the doorway. Her hair was loose to her shoulders, brushed and shining, and she was wearing a white summery dress with no sleeves and a soft, floaty skirt. She carried an apricot silk wrap, and her skin looked natural and free from make-up. She was…in a word…

Lovely…

Breathtakingly so.

And she looked as if she might, at any moment, burst into tears.

Seth cursed beneath his breath as he realised she'd overheard his conversation with Ming, and the comparison with Rachel. *Damn.* He'd meant it as a compliment, but it could just as easily have sounded like a put-down to her. Problem was, he couldn't explain exactly what he'd meant by his 'chalk and cheese' statement without embarrassing her in front of Ming, and without casting her best friend in a bad light.

Despite the abrupt and awkward silence, Amy came into the room and flashed a bright smile, clearly determined to carry on as if she'd heard nothing. 'Has Bella finished her dinner?'

'She's eaten every drop,' Seth told her.

'Ming, you must be a genius.' Amy admired the empty bowl elaborately. 'Bella doesn't normally eat much in the evenings.'

Ming grinned. 'Everyone likes my cooking.'

'You should thank Ming, Bella.'

'Thank you, Ming,' the little girl parroted obediently, but her smile was genuine enough to melt the shy cook's heart.

'Now drink up your milk because it's time for bed.'

As soon as the milk was down Amy whisked the child away.

Not once did she look at Seth.

Amy took a deep breath as she walked across the subtly lit veranda, past a table set prettily for two, with a candle under a glass dome and a pink ceramic bowl filled with floating flowers. She found Seth sitting on the top veranda step, staring out into the vast, moony black night.

'Seth?'

His head whipped around and his gaze was fierce.

She swallowed. 'Would you mind saying goodnight to Bella?' Smiling awkwardly, she explained, 'I'm afraid she won't settle without a kiss from you.'

'Sure.' He stood quickly and looked as uncomfortable as Amy felt.

'I'll wait here,' she said steadily, but she was fighting tears as she watched him go. It was so silly. She was upset on all sorts of levels tonight.

Bella's demand that Seth be the one to tuck her in had hurt. Amy hated to think she was jealous, but the little girl was falling for Seth fast and hard. She seemed to be totally fascinated by him—utterly trusting, excited and enthralled.

Amy told herself it was because Bella had very

little experience of men. Rachel had stopped going out with guys once she'd known she was pregnant, and, of course, Dominic had stayed well out of any scene that had involved Bella.

But now, it was almost as if Bella sensed that Seth was special, and connected to her. It was fanciful to think that the child knew he was her father. But very soon he would want her to know the truth, and, although she was too little to really understand, it would be an important step in cementing their emotional bond.

Leaving her wrap on the veranda railing, Amy leaned against a post and looked out at the inky sky where a silvery half-moon was glowing softly through a gap in the trees. She thought again about the conversation she'd overheard in the kitchen.

It was *really* silly to be upset about that. She knew very well she was different from Rachel. It was very true they were chalk and cheese. Their differences had kept their friendship in balance. But it was only logical that, if Seth had been madly attracted to cheese, he was unlikely to fall for chalk.

Of course she knew that.

She had never, in her wildest dreams, expected Rachel's ex to be interested in her. She just wished he hadn't held her hand this evening, hadn't made that one slow, deliberate stroke on her skin. She was quite, quite sure she would remember that slide of his thumb for the rest of her life.

*But how idiotic was that?*

Anyone would think she was a trembling virgin who'd been locked away in a tower for a hundred years and knew absolutely nothing about men. Truth be told, she'd had experience, but she had a terrible habit of picking the wrong kind of guy. Each relationship had ended unhappily.

If she had any brains she'd avoid men completely. How on earth had she allowed this man, this *highly unsuitable* man, to reduce her to such a pathetic state in such a short space of time?

She was a *fool*!

At the sound of Seth's footsteps, she spun around.

'All quiet on the nursery front,' he said, smiling.

'Is Bella asleep?'

'Just about.' He came and stood close beside Amy. 'And judging by the aromas coming from the kitchen, I'd say our dinner's almost ready.'

'Something smells amazing. Is it curry?'

'Seafood curry. One of Ming's specialties.'

'Wow. So we're in for a treat.'

On cue, Ming appeared with a bamboo tray holding a bowl of steaming jasmine rice and a large blue and white covered pot, which he placed in the centre of the table.

'Thanks, Ming,' Seth said with the very slightest hint of an amused smile and a courteous dip of his head.

'Enjoy.' Ming bestowed them both with an eloquent grin before disappearing discreetly.

Seth pulled out a chair for Amy and, to her dismay, the old-fashioned gesture set her heart speeding again.

She kept her gaze lowered as he sat opposite her and she told herself again to remember that she was the guardian of Bella's future. That was her role here.

It was time to forget the handholding, the

suntan, and the heavenly blue eyes. Seth was her host and she was his guest. No more, no less.

She took a deep breath and smelled their fragrant meal and the scent of frangipani. In the glow of the candlelight, Seth's shirt gleamed whitely and his throat was a dark shadow above the V of his open collar. She concentrated on safer things—the smooth gleam of silver cutlery, the crisp white napkins and the fine matchstick placemats dyed a deep watermelon pink.

Helping herself to fluffy spoonfuls of the aromatic rice and curry, she made a stab at polite conversation. 'I have to keep reminding myself that this is a cattle station,' she said. 'I feel as if I'm on holidays at a beautiful resort.'

'Well, this should be a holiday for you. I'm sure you deserve a break,' Seth said with a smile. 'But tomorrow I'll take you and Bella to see the rest of Serenity. You'll soon see there are plenty of cattle.'

'How many?'

'At the moment we have around seven thousand.'

Amy's eyebrows lifted. 'More than a few,

then.' Between mouthfuls, she added, 'This food is sensational.'

'Ming's outdone himself tonight.'

Seth looked and sounded amused, which confused her.

'Do you dine out here alone, when you don't have guests?'

He shook his head. 'Hans and Ming often join me here. Sometimes I eat in the kitchen, or over with the stockmen. It varies.'

'I wish I'd known that. I would have been more than happy for Hans and Ming to have joined us tonight.'

'What? And spoil their fun?'

Amy frowned.

'Those guys see so few women,' Seth explained, gesturing to the candle and the bowl of flowers. 'Hans adores his garden, and Ming loves his cooking, and they live for the chance to do this kind of thing.'

'But they probably think—'

'Relax. I've explained our situation to them.'

'What did you tell them?'

'That you're a friend of Rachel's. That you and Bella are in the north on business. Just passing through.'

Amy nodded, reassured. She wondered if Seth would tell the others about Bella's relationship to him once she was gone.

As she thought about their departure in a few days' time, she realised, with a start, how very far away Melbourne felt. Already, it was almost as if she'd lived there in another lifetime.

She looked out into the moonlit garden, to the dark wall of trees beyond, and the twinkling stars peeping above the forest canopy. This alternative reality had already wrapped itself around her senses. Her heart.

'I love these open verandas,' she said. 'They're such a good idea. Like living in the garden.'

'The best way to live in the tropics.'

'But what happens in bad weather? Don't you have cyclones here?'

'We have built-in storm shutters that roll down. This whole area can be made completely secure.'

'That's clever. Who designed that? Your uncle?'
Seth nodded.

'Was there a woman involved? It's all so—so lovely.'

'No woman. My uncle had a flair for design. He liked to be surrounded by beautiful things.'

A shadow crossed Seth's face like a cloud over the moon.

Ever so casually, Amy asked, 'Did Rachel stay here in this house when she was working here?'

Seth blinked and the cloud vanished. His eyes were suddenly bright and alert with more than a hint of wariness. 'No, Rachel stayed over in the barracks with the other staff.'

'I see.' Amy wasn't sure what to make of that information and she paid careful attention to her food.

'She also spent some time on one of the islands,' Seth said.

'With you?' Oh, good grief. Amy couldn't believe she'd asked such a pointed question, but now that it was out she couldn't take it back.

Seth, however, dodged her question with the

practised skill of a politician. 'She liked to take the dinghy across to Turtle Island on her days off,' he said. 'She liked the view to the west, looking back to the mainland, especially at sunset.'

'I suppose that's why she called her book *Northern Sunsets*.'

He lowered his gaze. 'I dare say.'

She could all too easily imagine Rachel with this highly desirable man, alone on a tropical island, watching the sunset, but the thought made her ridiculously miserable and her throat prickled painfully as she tried to swallow.

'Let's not talk about Rachel.' Seth was watching her carefully. 'I'm sure the memories must be upsetting for you.'

She nodded.

'I'd like to hear all about you.'

'Me?' Her head shot up and she stared at him. 'Why?'

As if the answer was obvious, he shrugged. 'You're Bella's guardian.'

'Oh, right. Yes, of course.' Why else would

Seth be interested in her? He had every right to check out his daughter's protector.

Tamping down the tiniest spurt of disappointment, Amy wondered where she should start.

'I know you work in marketing,' Seth prompted. 'Does that create difficulties for you with childcare?'

'I do some of my work from home,' she said defensively. 'But not all. Do you have a problem with day care?'

His eyes widened. 'I know very little about it. If you're single, I guess you don't have an option.'

'That's right. I don't have an option, but it's not a problem. There's a wonderful day-care centre quite near me, and I have a big, extended family so I have a great back-up team.'

'Is your family in Melbourne?'

She nodded. 'I have two older brothers, both married with kids. And my parents, of course. Aunts, uncles. We have tons of family gatherings—Christmas, birthdays, Easter, Mother's Day. You name it, we celebrate. Any excuse for a Ross family get-together.'

'Sounds like fun,' Seth said, but a tight note had crept into his voice.

Sensitive to his distinct lack of family, Amy took her enthusiasm down a notch. 'Most of our gatherings are fun. But big families can be claustrophobic at times.'

'How does your family feel about Bella?'

Was this a trick question? 'They adore her, of course.'

'Of course.' Seth's face was grim as he speared a piece of fish with his fork. 'And what about your boyfriend?'

Amy tried to keep her tone casual. 'What boyfriend?'

Seth's gaze locked with hers. 'There's got to be a boyfriend. A girl like you must have a host of admirers.'

She almost choked. 'I don't have anyone at the moment. There was someone, but it—it didn't work out.'

It was weird how quickly Dominic had faded from her thoughts. Did it mean she was shallow that, after two months of living with Bella, she rarely thought about him? Now, in Seth's company, she didn't want to think about Dominic at all.

In the glow of the flickering candle, Seth's eyes had turned such a deep blue she feared she might drown in them.

'If there's no boyfriend,' he said softly, 'why are you blushing?'

*Because of the way you're looking at me.*

'Amy?'

She chewed nervously at her lower lip, unwilling to admit to Bella's father the exact reason that had prompted Dominic's departure. If he knew Bella was involved he might try to persuade her to leave his daughter here.

'Did this man break your heart?'

'Is that any of your business?'

'I thought we were having an adult conversation.'

'Yes, we are.' She let out an impatient huff. 'Did he?'

'Break my heart? No. I—I don't think so.'

'You don't *think* so?' Seth skewered her with

a searching, no-holds-barred gaze. 'That isn't possible. If your heart was broken you'd know about it.'

'You sound as if you're speaking from experience.'

He shrugged, but didn't answer, and she realised with a sharp pang that it was true. Seth had been hurt badly and he still carried the scars.

With her eyes on the bowl of floating flowers, she forced herself to ask, 'Was it Rachel? Did she break your heart?'

'No, not Rachel. It was years ago—long before she came here.'

Puzzled, Amy looked up, but he smiled at her with a surprisingly gentle look that sent her pulse spiralling helplessly. At the same moment she caught a movement out of the corner of her eye and she turned to see Bella in her green and white pyjamas, coming towards them across the veranda.

'Baby.' Amy jumped to her feet. 'What are you doing out here?'

'I waked up.'

Hurrying to the little girl, Amy scooped her up quickly and hugged her close. She smelled warm and sleepy, and she was rubbing at her eyes with one fist while she clutched her pink pig with the other.

'You didn't kiss me goodnight,' Bella said with a hint of bossiness.

Aware that Seth was watching them, Amy tried to be stern. 'But you sent me to find Seth. You wanted him to kiss you.'

'Want you, too,' Bella said, sticking out her bottom lip stubbornly.

'If I take you back to bed now and give you a kiss, you must promise to go straight back to sleep.'

'Sef, too.'

'But you've already had a goodnight kiss from Seth.'

Bella looked mutinous 'Sef, too.'

Amy sent a helpless glance back to Seth, and saw that he was already on his feet.

'It's OK,' he said, coming towards them with a slow, easy smile. 'I can give Bella two kisses in one night.'

'Well, yes. Of course.' Amy hoped she didn't sound flustered.

He followed her to the bedroom, and she was far too aware of his presence as she turned on the lamp, and rearranged Bella's toys around her pillow, then helped the little girl into bed and retucked the sheets.

Sitting on the edge of the bed, she gave Bella's soft cheek a kiss. 'Night, night.' Gave her another hug. 'Don't let the bed bugs bite.'

She stood and shuffled in the narrow space between the twin beds to make room for Seth, who suddenly seemed enormously tall and broad shouldered. And excessively male.

Bella's eyes shone as he perched on the bed beside her and she grinned with delight as he kissed her.

'Goodnight, possum.' Gently, he tucked a strand of hair from her face. 'Now close your eyes.'

Bella obeyed.

'Sleep tight.'

As Seth stood up in the confined space his

shoulder bumped Amy's arm and heat flashed through her like a skyrocket taking off.

She struggled to sound calm as she spoke to Bella. 'I'm going to leave the lamp on for ten minutes, and you must go to sleep.'

Before the little girl could think up another reason to delay her, she turned and left the room, and Seth followed.

Outside, beyond the bedroom's closed door, she sent him a nervous smile. 'I do hope she actually nods off this time.'

'She's not used to this house yet,' he said smoothly.

Amy knew this was true, but his indulgent attitude surprised her.

'She's used to sleeping in strange beds,' she said, and then, to her annoyance, she blushed again.

Seth's eyes sparkled with poorly concealed amusement.

'What's so funny?' she snapped.

'I was thinking—' He paused, looking at her, and the light in his eyes made her chest squeeze tight. 'I was thinking that it wouldn't be fair if Bella gets all the kisses.'

Amy stopped breathing, and Seth took a step closer.

# CHAPTER SIX

SETH told himself it was a simple thing.

He was merely being playful, giving Amy a friendly and innocent kiss on the cheek just like the one he'd given Bella.

So it made no sense that, from the moment he touched her—merely brushed a wisp of her hair from her cheek—he felt fine, electric tremors all over his body.

Amy was standing still. Very still... *Too* still...standing with her eyes closed...

Seth could see the delicate blue veins on her eyelids, and he could smell faint traces of the jasmine soap she'd used in the shower. He focused on her smooth, soft cheek and tried to ignore the softer-than-soft bow of her lips, but, for some reason that made no sense at all, he didn't find his way to her cheek…

He dipped lower…

Until his mouth brushed against hers…and they shared a beat of trembling hesitation…and then a gentle, lingering touch…the most tender of hellos.

And Amy didn't pull away.

Seth felt a subtle increase in the pressure of her mouth against his, and then her lips parted, yielding and warm. She tasted of the summer night and his blood began to roar.

His heart pounded, his skin burned…the homestead veranda faded and the entire universe became Amy.

Sweetly erotic Amy.

Her mouth was so soft and warm, just how he knew it would be. Oh, God. He'd been fighting this attraction from the moment he saw her in the Tamundra pub, and now she was offering heaven…

He wanted nothing but this…. Amy, breathless and needy, her skin silky and hot under his hand.

Her kiss…was such a perfect thing…

But she went suddenly still and pulled away.
Seth realised that Ming was there.

'I—I've left your desserts ready in the kitchen,'
Ming said, eyes wide with poorly suppressed
delight, then he scuttled sideways like a crab
down the hallway, as if he couldn't hurry away
from them fast enough.

As Seth struggled to breathe he heard Amy's
voice calling, 'Thanks for dinner, Ming. The
seafood curry was sensational.'

She sounded astonishingly calm, not at all
like a woman who'd been drowning in a whirl-
pool of passion.

With her back very straight, her chin high, she
turned and sailed ahead of Seth onto the veranda,
leaving him reeling in her wake.

He took a swift, steadying breath. If there was
one thing he'd learned to do well, it was to hide
his feelings. No way did he want Amy to guess
how seriously he'd been rocked by that kiss.

Once they were out of Ming's earshot he
asked, almost calmly, 'Do you think Bella will
settle now?'

Amy stared at him blankly, as if she hadn't a clue what he was talking about. Hastily, she looked the other way. 'Sorry, what did you say? I—I w-was distracted.'

This was better. Perhaps they were on the same wavelength after all.

She lifted her hands in a nervous gesture of helplessness. 'I—I was hoping Ming hasn't got the wrong idea.'

'He's discreet, like all my staff.'

'Well, yes, I'm sure he is,' she said unhappily.

Seth opened his mouth to apologise, but swiftly changed his mind. He wasn't about to apologise for kissing a lovely girl in the moonlight.

And he wasn't prepared to admit that the kiss might have been a mistake, even though it was almost certainly a huge error of judgement. He'd let his desire for Amy complicate a situation that was already thorny enough. He would have to tell her the truth sooner rather than later, but he couldn't face it now. The painful story was still raw inside him. *I'll do it soon,* he thought. *When I've had more time to prepare.*

For now, he decided, it was better to simply change the subject.

'Are you ready for dessert?' Before Amy could object, Seth added, quickly, 'You have to try Ming's watermelon balls in green ginger wine.'

The ghost of a smile flickered. 'That does sound tempting.'

'Take a seat. I'll be back in a sec—as soon as I collect the desserts from the kitchen.'

As Seth headed off Amy let out her breath on a shuddering sigh. She felt as if she'd been holding her breath ever since he'd kissed her, and now she was grateful for this moment alone, for this chance to close her eyes while she relived that astonishing experience.

It was too bad that Ming had seen them, but she wasn't nearly as worried as she'd made out.

What she wondered now was how she'd lived so long, and dated so many guys, without discovering that one kiss could be a phenomenal, life-changing moment.

Gently, with a sense of wonderment, she traced

the soft skin on her lips as she remembered the hot, out-of-this-world thrill that had jolted through her body as Seth's mouth settled against hers.

She'd give anything to experience that sensation again—*everything*: her job, her life in Melbourne, the close contact with her family.

She'd never felt anything remotely as exciting when Dominic had kissed her. Small wonder their relationship hadn't survived. There'd been no real chemistry.

Chemistry. That was the secret ingredient in tonight's kiss, wasn't it? Mysterious, magical, astonishing chemistry.

But chemical reactions could also be dangerous and she had to remember that now as she heard Seth's footsteps returning.

She had to remember that Seth was potentially dangerous. Chances were, every woman reacted that way when he kissed them. Especially that one woman who'd broken his heart.

*And Rachel.*

A thud of disappointment brought Amy back to earth. What on earth had she been thinking?

She couldn't afford to forget, even for a moment, why she was here. Clearly, this man was indeed dangerous. He had seduced her best friend and made her pregnant and here she was getting into a flap over a tiny kiss that probably meant nothing more to him than yet another woman falling at his feet.

'I think you'll find this dessert is the perfect second course after curry,' Seth said as he reached her.

'Thank you,' she said primly.

He set a green glass bowl in front of her and she caught the sweet scent of watermelon mingled with the deeper spiciness of the green ginger wine.

'That smell reminds me of Christmas,' she said, determined to steer her thoughts onto a safer track.

'It certainly reminds me of summer. Tuck in.'

She watched as Seth slipped a marble-sized ball of lush pink fruit from his spoon to his mouth.

*Oh, for heaven's sake!* Already she was thinking about his mouth, about his kiss—so perfect.

'What's Christmas like here?' she asked, trying again for a distraction. 'Do you usually have a big party?'

'Not any more. We used to throw parties, but they're not really my scene.'

'That's a pity.' She looked around her at the open-plan living spaces on the veranda, and she pictured paper lanterns in the garden. 'This is a perfect house for a party, and with Ming to help with catering it would be a breeze, and so much fun.'

'So you like parties, do you?'

'Most parties,' she said. 'I sometimes have to organise them as part of my job—to help clients with networking, or to launch new products.'

As she said this Amy was hit by memories of the launch party on the night Rachel died and she felt another sickening thud, deep inside, as if her heart had crashed from a great height.

'Amy, are you all right?'

She reached for her water glass and took a deep sip. 'I'm OK,' she said. 'It just catches me every so often—the pain, you know—when I think about Rachel.'

'Yeah,' he said softly. 'I do know what you mean. And it lasts a long time, I'm afraid. I still miss my dad after all these years, and it's been worse since my uncle died.'

She was surprised that Seth hadn't mentioned mourning for Rachel, too. Surely he must feel some degree of grief for Bella's mother?

For Amy the smallest memory of Rachel could trigger pain—Rachel's habit of flicking her long, pale hair over her shoulders. Her deep, throaty laugh. A punchline from the zany jokes she loved to tell.

But she wasn't prepared to share these memories with Seth. It was far safer to leave the intimate details of his history with Rachel where they belonged—firmly in the past.

Unhappily, she scooped up a spoonful of wine-drenched fruit. 'Can you tell me more about your uncle? Did he always live here?'

Seth shook his head. 'He started off in Sydney like the rest of my family. Moved to Cape York in his late twenties.'

'To be a cattleman?'

'Yeah.' Seth smiled. 'Left a thriving family business to become a struggling grazier.'

'That's intriguing.' She dipped her spoon into the bowl. These watermelon balls were amazing. 'What was the family business?'

'Have you ever heard of Reardon and Grace?'

She shook her head.

'It's a very old importing and exporting business. My great-great-grandfather started it way back, and he owned one of the first warehouses in Sydney.'

'Wow.'

'All the men in my family have played a role in the firm, including my father. Seth was the first to leave.'

'Seth? Was that your uncle's name, too?'

'Yes. He was my father's younger brother.'

Amy frowned. Somehow, this information seemed significant, but she was too caught up in this story to stop and puzzle it out. 'Why did he leave Sydney?'

Seth's mouth twisted into a wry smile and she winced.

'Am I being too nosy?'

'Not really.' His steady gaze met hers. 'But it's rather a sad tale.'

Unwilling to push him, she took another spoonful of her dessert.

'You see, my uncle was madly in love,' Seth said quietly. 'And everything was fine until he brought his girlfriend home and introduced her to his older brother.'

'To your father?'

He nodded. 'He wasn't my father then, of course. This was before I was born.'

'But your father fell in love with the same woman as your uncle?'

'Yes, and he married her.'

The penny dropped, making Amy gasp. 'So this woman was your mother. Your uncle was in love with your mother.'

'Completely and hopelessly, I'm afraid.'

'The poor man.'

Amy could picture it all. Seth's uncle, this other Seth Reardon, must have been so upset when he lost the woman he loved, that he'd left his comfortable life in Sydney and travelled all the way up here to try to forget her. To start a new life.

'Did he have to start here from scratch?' she asked.

'More or less. It was hard work, but he took to the life like he was born and bred for it, and he soon toughened up. You know what they say? When the going gets tough, the tough get going. He pitched in with the fencing gangs. Joined in the mustering. Helped to build this house. He thrived on the life here.'

'But he never married?'

'No.' Seth's brow furrowed in a deep frown. 'When my father died, my mother brought me here, and I think my uncle had hoped that she'd stay.'

'But she went to America?'

'Chasing her dream.' His face darkened. 'This is no life for a woman.'

'Why couldn't a woman live here?' Amy asked. 'It's beautiful.'

'The house and garden might be beautiful,' Seth said tersely. 'But that's all there is here to keep a woman happy. There are no shops or cafés. No chance for catching up with girl-friends. The nearest hairdresser is in Cairns.'

Amy wanted to disagree. She knew Serenity was remote, but she suspected that a woman could be very happy here. She would have to be the right woman, of course, with the right man.

But if the two of them loved each other deeply, if the chemistry was right, why couldn't they be blissfully happy?

It wasn't a question she could ask when Seth's mother and Rachel and possibly the girl who'd broken his heart had not been prepared to stay.

Amy shivered at the thought of Seth's loneli-ness, which he seemed to accept as his fate. She longed to reach out and touch him tenderly, to cup her hand against the rugged line of his jaw, to brush his lips with the pad of her thumb, to show him that she cared.

She longed to rekindle the passion of their kiss, and now, with no Ming to interrupt them, who knew where it might lead? Amy didn't care. She wanted it, wanted him.

*But that's crazy.*

Oh, God. For an insane minute there, she'd almost forgotten Rachel, Bella, her job, her family... She'd almost been ready to throw every responsibility to the four winds...in exchange for a night with Seth.

Shaking, shocked by her foolishness, she reached across the table for his empty bowl. She spoke carefully. 'Thank you for the delicious meal. I'll take these things through to the kitchen.'

Instantly he was on his feet. 'No, you don't have to worry about the kitchen. You're a guest.'

Avoiding the fire in his gaze, she said, 'But I haven't performed a single helpful task since I arrived. Let me rinse these couple of bowls to keep my hand in.'

He gave her a puzzled smile. 'If you insist.'

'I insist,' she said quietly but emphatically. 'Goodnight, Seth.' She walked away swiftly, carrying the dishes, unable to return his smile.

A noise woke Amy, a sudden flapping of wings outside her room and the haunting call of a bird, which she thought must have been an owl. She rolled over and looked through the moon-streaked darkness to Bella's bed, hoping the sound hadn't woken her.

Fortunately, the little girl remained very still, undisturbed. Amy rolled onto her back again and closed her eyes. She crossed her fingers, hoping she would drift back to sleep.

She was tired. Really tired. She hadn't slept well since she'd left Melbourne and right now she wanted to stay drowsy and dopey. She needed to sleep, and not to think.

But already she could feel her brain whirring to fretful life, spinning thoughts…throwing up questions…

About…Seth.

And that kiss…

It was so easy now, in the middle of the night, to let her mind zoom in on the details of that kiss, to live it again in close focus.

She could feel again the intimate brush of his lips against hers, the imprint of his hand at the small of her back, the nerve-tingly pleasure and the rush of delicious heat that had flooded her, the astonishing need, the glorious, overwhelming longing…

Good grief. She was going mad, wasn't she? She had to be a little crazy to get into such a fever about one kiss.

From the start, she'd sensed she should be wary of Seth Reardon. He was incredibly sexy, despite or perhaps because of his remote, brooding air, but she'd picked up all kinds of signals that he was dangerous, too.

Rachel had been so cagey about him. Even the woman at the Tamundra pub had hinted that he was trouble. And on reflection Amy had to admit she'd had difficulty thinking straight from the moment she'd met him.

Thank heavens she hadn't thrown herself at him tonight.

The man was a disturbing mystery.

He'd claimed that his heart had been broken, but it hadn't happened over Rachel.

And yet…he'd made love to Rachel and she'd thought he was *The One*…and he'd fathered

Bella, and now Rachel was dead…but Seth wasn't particularly upset about it.

None of it made sense. Had the man no feelings?

Was there a cold unemotional side to him that Amy hadn't seen yet? Had Rachel known that, and sensibly kept her distance?

With a groan Amy rolled over to face the wall and thumped at her pillow. The Seth she'd seen over the past two days had given her the impression that he was warm and vulnerable—and wounded—but that didn't sit with the alternative image of him as cold and unfeeling.

Would the real Seth Reardon please stand up?

He was a jigsaw puzzle she couldn't solve unless she found the vital missing pieces.

She'd wanted to ask him about the woman who'd broken his heart, but she didn't know him well enough to ask such an intimate question. She'd known him for such a short time.

Heavens, had it really only been two days?

Sighing heavily, Amy rolled the other way again and pulled the sheet around her bare shoulders. She thought about Seth's uncle's sad story, and she wondered how the poor man had felt when Seth's mother—the woman he'd loved and lost—had given his name to her son.

And how had he felt years later, when his young nephew had been abandoned by that woman? He'd probably taken care of the younger Seth out of love for his brother, and a sense of duty, but it must have hurt deeply, if he'd still loved the boy's mother, in spite of her failings.

But fancy there being two Seth Reardons. That was a surprise. That was—

*Oh, my God.*

Amy shot upright in the bed, her heart racing.

It was a crazy thought, but…

Was it possible…was it even remotely possible that Seth's *uncle* had been Rachel's lover?

When Seth told her that his uncle had died, she'd pictured him as an elderly man, but he needn't have been *that* old.

At a guess, she would say that Seth was around thirty, and his uncle was younger than Seth's father, so he might have been only fifty or so when Rachel met him.

She tried to imagine Rachel falling for a fifty-year-old man. He'd need to have been a well-preserved and decidedly good-looking fifty-year-old man—but he was sure to be handsome if he was related to Seth.

It was possible, wasn't it?

Her friend had always been a little unconventional in her tastes, and the more Amy thought about it, the more it started to make sense.

Rachel was less likely to burden an older man with the news that he was about to become a father. She'd confided to Amy that her schooldays had been blighted by the fact that her parents were so much older than everyone else's folks. Kids were cruel and their barbed comments had hurt.

And if Seth's uncle had fathered Bella, the younger Seth's apparent lack of grief for Rachel made more sense, too.

Slowly Amy sank back onto the pillow.

Wow!

Her head reeled with the thought that the Seth she knew, the Seth who'd kissed her and sent her to the moon, might not be Bella's father after all. It was ridiculous, but she *loved* the possibility that he hadn't been Rachel's lover.

*But hang on, girl. Don't jump to too many conclusions.*

This could be wishful thinking. If Seth wasn't Bella's father, why hadn't he just come out and said so? Was he trying to protect his uncle? His reputation? Was that why he'd been so negative about Rachel's book?

Or was her new theory total rubbish?

Amy groaned. She wouldn't be able to get any of these answers until morning, but the questions were going to keep her awake all night.

Seth woke, as he always did, at dawn and he lay very still, with his eyes closed, listening to the silence of the sleeping house and to the warbling songs of the honeyeaters in the rainforest, signalling the start of a new day.

Out of habit, he reached for the wristwatch on his bedside table and squinted at its dial. Yep. Five-twenty a.m. on the dot.

Normally he would leap out of bed. In summer, he liked to get any heavy work out of the way before the day got too hot. But in deference to his houseguests, he stayed put. They were just across the hall and the slightest sound might disturb them. No point in waking them too early.

It had made sense, he'd thought, to put Amy and Bella together in the room across the hall. If the little girl was scared during the night, Amy would be there for her.

But he couldn't help fantasising about Amy sleeping in a room on her own…

*OK, lamebrain, what could you have done? Snuck into her room? Continued on where the kiss left off? Oh, yeah. Brilliant. Then you'd really make a dog's breakfast of this tricky situation.*

If only he could stop thinking about her. Memories of their brief kiss had haunted him all night, reappearing and expanding out of all proportion in a string of X-rated dreams.

He wasn't sure that he could survive too many nights with Amy in his house, sleeping in her flimsy white nightdress just across the hallway. He'd be a pile of cinders before the time was up.

Problem was, the wanting wasn't only about physical desire.

He'd found himself enjoying simply *being* with Amy…hanging out…talking with her and listening to the warmth in her voice…watching the changing moods in her lovely brown eyes… admiring the sweet and tender way she cared for Bella.

For years, Seth had avoided this level of interest in any one woman, but Amy Ross had slipped quietly under his radar. She was so easy to be with and there was something delightfully refreshing about her. He liked her *and* he desired her, and he couldn't stop thinking about her.

*Damn it…* He had to stop.

He knew he and Amy had no future. Hadn't he learned anything from Jennifer?

His gaze flickered again to the nightstand and he saw the fancy wristwatch that had been Jennifer's last gift, the precious farewell gift she given him before she went back to New York.

She'd been so excited about finding the watch in a jewellery shop in Cairns.

'It tells two different time zones simultaneously, so you'll always know what time it is in New York. Isn't that neat, Seth? You'll know the right time to call, and you'll be able to picture what I'm doing. I won't be so far away.'

'But it can't change the facts, Jen,' he'd warned her. 'You'll still be on the other side of the world.'

'I'll come back. Soon. I promise.'

With that promise calming his fears, they'd made love for the last time, and if Seth closed his eyes he could still see the morning sunlight rimming Jennifer's auburn hair with fire…could still see the rainbow flashes from the diamond he'd put on her finger.

He'd let her go home.

To America.

She'd been so sure she would simply wind things up in New York and come hurrying back to marry him.

'I love you, Seth. I promise, darling. I don't need the city, when I'm with you.'

*I promise…*

She'd been sincere at the time—he'd give her that. Jennifer had never dreamed she would find the pull of her hometown impossible to resist. In all innocence, he'd let her go back and, inevitably, she'd been seduced by the exciting bustle and buzz of the Big Apple. She'd found herself clinging once more to the security of familiar faces, to the reassurance of well-loved sights and sounds, to the comfort of crowds.

It had only taken six weeks before she'd come to her senses. She'd cried so hard when she'd telephoned Seth that he'd barely been able to make out a word she was saying, but eventually he'd understood that she wasn't coming back, and, no, he shouldn't fly over there to be with her.

It couldn't work, she told him. Their worlds were too different.

For Seth, the lesson was clear.

Love, alone, was not enough.

The softest breath fanned Seth's cheek. Startled, he turned to find Bella's blue eyes half an inch from his.

'What are you doing here, little one?'

'Up!' the little girl demanded, and before he realised quite what was happening she gripped his bed sheets, slung one leg high and hauled herself, like a tiny commando, up into the bed beside him.

'Should you be here?' he asked as he flung one hand out to prevent her from tumbling back to the floor. 'Where's Amy?'

Bella didn't answer.

Somewhat alarmed, he scooted over to make room for her in his king-sized bed. She merely giggled and began to bounce on the mattress, sending her dark curls flying.

She was a cutie—no doubt about that—this tiny human being who was, amazingly, related to him.

Seth knelt on the bed, ready to catch her if she bounced too high, and he marvelled at her incredible energy and enthusiasm. She was such a happy little thing, so full of life, and, thanks to Amy, she had no sense of the tragedies that had robbed her of her parents.

The word orphan had always horrified Seth.

When his father died and his mother disappeared to the far side of the world, he'd been haunted by visions of storybook orphans, starving and freezing in the snow.

But he'd had his mother's letters. Inadequate, but tangible, they'd arrived on his birthdays—and he'd had his uncle, whose kindness and love had saved him and kept him afloat.

Now, as he watched this giggling, bouncing little girl, he choked up, thinking about the man who'd fathered her.

*I owe you one, mate. I owe you big time.*

Except that Amy had picked up the baton. She'd assumed responsibility for her friend's daughter and, as far as Seth could tell, she loved the kid unreservedly, as if she were her own.

He supposed the security and stability of Amy's happy family had given her the grounding she needed to reach out without fear. Seemed she was doing damn fine splendid and she didn't need his help.

'You're a lucky kid,' he told Bella. 'You're much better off with her.'

\* \* \*

Within seconds of waking, Amy saw that Bella's bed was empty.

She bounced out of bed in a panic. Bella usually climbed straight into Amy's bed for a morning cuddle and she'd never wandered off before.

Amy darted into the hallway. 'Bella!'

'She's in here.'

In mid-dash down the hallway, Amy skidded to a halt. Seth's voice had come from his bedroom.

*Zap.* Heart thumping, she turned in at his doorway.

Part of her brain must have registered that Bella was bouncing in the middle of Seth's huge bed, but almost all of her attention was caught by his bare chest.

*Oh, help.*

Amy had to stare; she simply *had* to. Seth's chest was so fabulously toned, so amazingly muscly and masculine and *naked.*

The sight of him now in his bedroom was such a different matter from seeing him by the pool yesterday. It was totally unexpected, for one thing. But now, after he'd kissed her… After her night of restless tossing and turning…

'Bella marched in here and took over my bed,' Seth explained, with an apologetic grin that didn't quite hide the fact that he was checking Amy out.

It was only when she saw the unmistakable spark of appreciation in his eyes that she remembered she was in her nightdress. Her thin white cotton nightdress. Again. Which meant she was even more scantily clad than he was.

This was becoming an embarrassing habit.

Surreptitiously, she attempted to cross her arms over her chest as she backed out of the room. 'Bella has so much energy first thing in the morning. Thanks for taking care of her.'

Frantically, she tried to beckon to the little girl. 'Come on, now, Bella. That's enough bouncing. Time to get dressed.'

Bella continued to bounce.

'Hey!' Seth caught the little girl in mid bounce and swept her so high she squealed with delight.

Amy watched the rippling sheen of his muscles and felt the oxygen sucked from her lungs.

Grinning, Seth turned to her, holding the giggling, wriggling child. 'Here you go. She's all yours.'

Struggling to breathe, she prepared to take Bella from him. Their forearms bumped, of course, and for a heady moment she found her hands squashed between Bella's squirming body and the solid wall of Seth's bare chest.

He was warm and satiny and hard…and touchable… She could feel his heat, smell his skin…

Pulling away, she blushed hotly, and turned to dash for the safety of her room, but she was distracted by a silver-framed photograph on the dresser near the door.

Clutching Bella, Amy took a second look. It was a close-up portrait of an incredibly handsome man approaching middle age.

His dark hair was feathered with silver and his face had the kind of tan that came from years of living in the outdoors. White creases showed at the corner of his eyes, but, despite the slightly weathered look, there was a breathtaking, film-star quality about him.

'Is this your uncle?' she asked.

Seth's eyes followed the direction of her gaze and she saw a flash of pain in their blue depths. 'Yes,' he said. 'That's Seth. Everyone around here called him Boss, so there was no confusion about our names.'

'He looks younger than I expected. When was the photo taken?'

'A few years ago. Not long before he died, actually.'

Cold shivers skittered down Amy's spine. So…Uncle Seth had been a hunk. A mature hunk certainly, but indisputably attractive.

Deep down, she sensed the truth as clearly as if the words had been spoken. This uncle had been Rachel's grand passion.

'Now's not the time, Seth, but you and I need to have a talk,' she said tightly. 'A serious talk.' Then she turned and fled from his room.

# CHAPTER SEVEN

AMY arrived on the veranda, half an hour later, dressed for breakfast and ready for a showdown.

The questions about Bella's father had to be answered.

Today. Preferably, this morning. She had no idea why Seth had remained silent and mysterious about Bella's conception, but she was determined to have everything out in the open.

Perhaps he'd guessed what was on her mind. Despite his smooth smile, she could sense an extra tension in him. *Good,* she thought. It wouldn't hurt for him to stew for a while; a little discomfort might make him more cooperative.

Guiltily conscious that she was thinking like an interrogator, Amy turned her attention to breakfast, which was another of Ming's masterpieces.

While Amy helped Bella to dip toast soldiers into her softly boiled egg, she talked to Seth as any guest might, about the fruit trees scattered about the garden, and the hens in the coop at the back of the house.

'Perhaps Bella and I could collect the eggs,' she suggested. 'You'd like that, wouldn't you, poppet?'

'You're very welcome to collect them,' Seth told her. 'I'll warn Ming that the job's covered for the next few days.'

Playing his part as host, Seth talked politely and carefully about the scenic spots around the property. Amy was equally polite as she tried to pay attention, but she found it hard when her brain was boiling with seriously important questions.

As soon as Bella finished her breakfast Amy grabbed her chance. 'Seth, do you think Ming could keep Bella entertained, while we have half an hour to ourselves?'

He gave an unsmiling nod and stood. 'Ming's a good sport. I'll speak to him. I'm sure he'll oblige.'

In no time, Ming appeared, dark eyes sparkling

as he flashed Amy a wide grin. 'Does Bella like to blow bubbles?'

She couldn't help laughing. 'Do kangaroos hop? Bella, would you like to blow bubbles?'

The little girl squealed, and as easily as that she was whisked away to the kitchen.

And Amy was alone with Seth.

'More tea?' he asked, smiling enigmatically as he lifted the teapot.

'Thanks.'

She had to concentrate hard, keeping her hand steady as Seth filled her teacup and his, then set the pot down. He regarded her steadily. 'You said we need to talk.'

'Yes, I did.' Amy took her time adding milk to her tea while she marshalled her thoughts. She had to get this right, had to get to the truth without making Seth angry.

Over the rim of his teacup, he watched her. 'Am I right in guessing you have questions?'

'Quite a few questions, actually,' she said. 'And I hope you'll give me straight answers.'

His expression remained impassive. 'Fire away.'

This was it. Time to hold her nose and jump in. 'Are you Bella's father?'

Seth looked her straight in the eyes. 'No, Amy. I'm not.'

*Oh, boy.* She felt as if she'd dived into a pool only to discover too late that it was the shallow end. Even though she'd guessed this possibility, it was still a shock to have it confirmed. 'You— you know that for sure?'

'Absolutely. I didn't sleep with Rachel. In fact, I had very little to do with her while she was here.'

*I didn't sleep with Rachel.*

Amy sat very still, trying to ignore the warm wave of relief that rippled through her. It was totally inappropriate to be pleased simply because this gorgeous man hadn't made love to her best friend.

She had to forget the way her body went into meltdown at his slightest touch. Her focus was Bella—Bella's parentage. Bella's future.

Bella was the only reason these questions were important. If Amy was going to take care of Bella for the next eighteen years or so, she

wanted everything about Bella's family background out in the open. No murky secrets or
skeletons in the cupboard.

'Rachel told me that Bella's father was Seth
Reardon, so I assumed you were—'

'The culprit?'

'Yes.' With one finger, she traced the teacup's
handle. 'But if it's not you I suppose Bella's
father was—the other Seth.'

He nodded slowly. 'Your friend and my uncle
were lovers. Neither my uncle nor I knew of Bella's
existence, but if Rachel named Seth Reardon as her
father, I can only assume Bella's their child.'

So there was the truth at last—or as close to the
truth as she was ever going to get.

Amy folded her arms and hugged them against
her, needing a little head space to adjust to this
news. Rachel's lover was not *this* Seth Reardon,
but a wonderfully attractive, older man. A man
who, like Rachel, was no longer alive.

'Poor little Bella,' she said.

'She's fine, Amy.'

'But she has no mother or father.'

'She has you. You're a terrific mother. You're doing a fantastic job.'

She shrugged uneasily—disappointed that she couldn't feel happier now that she'd achieved her goal. 'Why didn't you tell me? Why did you let me think you were Bella's father?'

Seth switched his gaze to a distant spot in the garden. 'Would you like to go for a walk?'

*A walk? He wanted to take a walk now?*

'Are you trying to lead me up the garden path, Seth?'

He gave a soft laugh. 'No, but I can explain things better outside.'

She shrugged uncertainly. 'All right.' She supposed he mightn't want Ming to overhear them.

As they went down the short flight of timber steps the air was warm and humid and laden with the scent of frangipani. They followed a flagstone path past a bed of lush green plants with astonishing bright orange flowers shaped like lobster claws, and Amy stole a glance at Seth's frowning face.

She wasn't going to be put off. Now that she'd adjusted, she was getting increasingly angry that he'd let her think the wrong thing for so long. 'Were you ever going to tell me about your uncle?' she asked.

'I was planning to tell you the whole story.'

'When?' she snapped, annoyed by his coolness. 'When Bella turns twenty-one?'

His mouth tightened and, to her dismay, a distressing sheen brightened his cobalt eyes.

Sudden sympathy burned her throat and she stopped walking. She knew Seth had loved his uncle. 'I'm sorry,' she said gently. 'I should remember that this is difficult for you, too.'

They were at the top of a long flight of stone steps that led down to the very bottom of the garden. Below the steps, the tangle of scrub began, but right in front of them lay a breathtaking view of the beach below, curling like a slice of lemon peel at the edge of the sparkling, dancing sea.

'I always intended to tell you the truth,' Seth said. 'That's why I brought you back here. But I felt it was important to get to know you first, to make sure I was doing the right thing. And I wanted you to see this place, so you had the whole picture.'

Amy looked at the sea, shimmering like aquamarine silk. She looked at the moss-green islands floating silently, then she looked back to the beautiful house, the terraced gardens, the dark forest of trees. She thought about the hundreds of hectares beyond this, all of which had belonged to Bella's father.

'You're right,' she said. 'Seeing this place has certainly opened my eyes. It's nothing like I expected. I suppose you have to be wary of people turning up out of the blue and claiming some kind of connection. Like land rights. But that's not why I've come here, Seth. I simply wanted to find Bella's…family. Her roots.'

'I know,' he said quietly. 'And for my part, I'm very happy to have found Bella. I need family too and she's incredibly important to me. My relatives are rather thin on the ground.'

He flashed Amy a lopsided smile and her bones threatened to melt.

He said, 'Some time in the future, you'll be able to tell Bella all about this place.'

*Some time in the future…*

She thought about going back to Melbourne and resuming her old life…

Before she'd left the city, she'd wanted nothing more than to hurry back there as soon as this mission was accomplished. But from the moment she'd first set eyes on Seth in Tamundra, she'd been foolishly losing her sense of direction.

Even if they hadn't shared that sensational kiss last night, she'd still be in danger of swooning whenever he was near. Every moment she spent with him she was falling a little more deeply under his spell.

*Newsflash, Amy. The enchantment is one sided.*

Seth's kiss might have bowled her over, but it was a mere blip on *his* radar. He'd shown no interest in an encore.

It was time to be sensible. She had to stick to the original plan, which meant finding out as much as she could about Bella's father, then heading straight for home.

'There's something down here that I should show you while we're talking,' Seth said, and he began to descend the stone steps.

Amy kept pace beside him. 'Can you tell me more about your uncle and Rachel?'

His hesitation was momentary. 'I can tell you that he loved her. I didn't realise it straight away, but he was head over heels.'

Amy nodded, recognising the familiar story. Guys were often falling head over heels for Rachel—except that this time, Rachel hadn't remained immune.

'Apparently, this was the first time my uncle had been so deeply in love since he met my mother,' Seth said.

They'd reached the bottom of the steps and she saw a track winding through the untamed scrub. Seth slowed his pace.

'I think Rachel felt the same way,' Amy told him. 'For ages, she wouldn't talk about her baby's father, and that was highly unusual for her. Finally she admitted that she loved him, but she didn't think she could live here. Do you think your uncle tried to persuade her to stay?'

'I'm sure he must have. He certainly didn't want her to leave.'

'But he didn't try to come after her either.'

Seth stopped walking. His mouth was a pensive downward curve and he stood with his thumbs hooked through the belt loops of his jeans, not quite meeting Amy's gaze. 'I know he was worried that he couldn't make the relationship work, but he still wanted to jump on a plane and fly down to Rachel.'

His mouth twisted unhappily. 'I'm afraid I persuaded him that he shouldn't try to follow her.'

'Why?'

Her abrupt question seemed to anger him. 'Seth was a fifty-year-old man chasing after a girl almost half his age.'

'Stranger things have happened in the name of love.'

'Love?' He sent her a sharp glance.

'Why are you looking at me like that?'

'I don't want to bad-mouth your friend…'

He left the sentence dangling and now it was Amy who was angry. 'What?' she demanded. 'What are you not telling me?'

'I—I wasn't convinced that Rachel really cared

for my uncle.' He looked away, eyes squinted against the bright morning sun. 'She was a flirt. A girl on the lookout for a holiday fling.'

Telltale wariness flickered in his eyes.

Amy gasped. 'Don't tell me she flirted with you, too?'

Seth sighed heavily.

'Seth?'

'She made it pretty obvious she was interested.'

*Oh.*

It was pathetic, but Amy couldn't hold back her next question. 'But you didn't sleep with her, did you?'

'I told you, no.'

With a pained grimace he kicked at a stone and sent it tumbling down the track. 'Rachel arrived here full of flirtatious smiles and ready for fun, but I must admit she changed her tune after she met my uncle. But I still didn't recognise how deeply he was involved. I kept trying to downplay the romance. We went through this weird kind of role reversal, where he was the reckless, love struck kid and I was the cautioning adult.'

Cords of tension stood out on Seth's neck, and when he shoved tightly fisted hands into his jeans' pockets, knotted veins showed in his forearms.

'Seth, I didn't mean to pry. You don't have to—'

He kept talking as if he hadn't heard her. 'He came to me one morning in the middle of the wet season. We'd had really heavy rain and the roads were cut and he demanded that I fly him to Cairns. Come hell or high water, he was going to Melbourne. He still hadn't heard from Rachel—no phone calls, letters, or emails.'

Seth gave a despairing shake of his head. 'I told him he was a hot-headed fool, that he hadn't thought everything through. I said he should wait till the wet season was over. If he still felt the same way about her then, he should go.'

Again, Seth looked unhappily out to the distant green islands. 'I forgot how stubborn and independent he could be, and there's no fool like an old fool. He took off alone in the flaming tinny to go to Cairns by sea—'

'What's a tinny?'

'An aluminium dinghy. We used it for fishing around the islands, but my uncle was planning to take it all the way to Cairns.' Seth's throat worked. 'A damn storm came up out of nowhere.'

Amy stared at him in dawning horror, guessing what would come next.

Grim-faced, Seth told her. 'A fishing trawler found the wreck three days later.'

The news rocked Amy. She'd never dreamed…

'I'm sure Rachel didn't know,' she whispered.

Appalled, she recognised Seth's grief, and felt his pain. It was there in the way he held himself stiffly, *so* stiffly, and his hurting was a live thing, reaching out to her and squeezing her heart.

'I blame myself,' Seth said softly. 'My uncle asked me to do one simple thing for him and I turned him down. After everything he'd done for me.'

Again, he kicked at a stone and, with a gruff, anguished growl, he began to stride away from Amy. She hurried down the track to catch up.

'You mustn't blame yourself,' she said.

He whirled around. 'Why not? I should have

seen how desperate he was. If I'd had any idea he'd take that bloody boat, I'd have flown him to Cairns in a heartbeat.'

Tears stung her eyes.

'I didn't know Rachel was pregnant.' His voice was rough and choked. 'I didn't know how to contact her after he died, but if I'd known she was pregnant, I would have made a bigger effort to find her.'

Blinking tears, Amy reached out and touched him on the arm.

He tensed as if she'd burned him.

'I do know how you feel, Seth.'

His eyes blazed with sudden anger. 'How could you possibly know?'

'I've been there. In that same place.'

She knew he didn't believe her, or care. His jaw hardened and a merciless light crept into his eyes. 'OK, so how do I feel?'

Amy's throat was tight, and it felt raw and fiery when she tried to swallow. 'You'd give anything to have that time over again, to make different choices.'

Seth continued to glare at her.

'Believe me, Seth, I know exactly what it feels like to be full of remorse, to feel responsible for what's happened. I've suffered all kinds of guilt over Rachel.'

In silence, he absorbed this news, and at last Amy saw his shoulders relax. He shook his head. 'But you weren't to blame for Rachel's accident.'

'I was,' she said, blinking back tears. 'I should have invited my boyfriend to a corporate launch, but I asked Rachel to come instead. If I hadn't invited her, if I'd asked Dominic and left Rachel safely at home with Bella, she'd still be alive.'

'But her accident was just bad luck. You told me that when you rang. Some fool ran a red light.'

Amy's stomach lurched unhappily and she couldn't look at him. She hated making this admission, but it had been eating at her for the past two months.

'I can't stop feeling guilty about that night because…because I wanted to show off to her. If I'm brutally honest, that was the real, the *only* reason I invited Rachel.'

Still she couldn't look at him, and she forced her eyes extra wide to hold her tears at bay. 'Rachel was always so amazingly clever and I finally had the chance to show her how good I was at *my* job. The launch party was going to be fabulous and I wanted her to see me in my finest hour. I—I can't believe I was so full of myself.'

She pressed her lips together tightly to hold back a sob.

'You're looking at this the wrong way,' Seth said, lifting his voice above the sudden noise of squabbling parrots in nearby trees. 'There's nothing wrong with inviting a best friend to a party.'

'But my motives were selfish.'

'So you wanted to show off? That's not exactly a crime, Amy. Half the parties in the world are about showing off.'

He snagged a stem of long grass and she found herself watching the deft movements of his fingers as he wove the strip of green into a narrow plait. A sigh escaped her.

'Perhaps we're both being too hard on ourselves,' he said quietly.

Was he right? She felt a tenuous but amazingly deep connection to him in this moment. Here were the two of them—grieving and alone, lost and guilty—two strangers from different worlds linked by one tiny girl.

'I know one thing,' she said, at last. 'No matter how badly we want to, we can't change what's happened.'

Seth nodded. 'All we can do is look for a way to move forward again.'

His eyes regarded her warmly. 'Speaking of moving on, I still haven't shown you why I brought you down here.'

'Do we have time? Shouldn't we get back to Bella?'

'This will only take a moment.'

Ahead of them, the track narrowed and Seth led the way, holding back giant fern fronds so they didn't brush against Amy. She heard the sound of running water and when they rounded the next bend, the track opened up to reveal a picture-perfect, fern-fringed rock pool fed by a cascading waterfall.

'Oh, wow!'

'It's an alternative swimming hole,' Seth said with a grin. 'Better than the beach because it's too high up for crocodiles.'

'It's beautiful.' It was *truly* beautiful. Even so, at the mention of crocodiles, Amy sent a cautious glance over the tumble of rocks and she quickly scanned the massive overhanging tree branches. 'Do snakes come here?'

'Not often.'

She edged closer to Seth. 'How often is not often?'

He grinned. 'I've seen the occasional harmless python sunning itself on a rock, but that's all.'

'But it wouldn't be safe to bring Bella here?'

'Why not? She'd be fine—as long as she was with a responsible adult. I wouldn't have brought you here if I thought it was dangerous.'

Amy turned from the pool to face him. 'You do understand how important Bella is to me, don't you? Rachel was my best friend and now you know how I feel about the accident—'

'You want to make amends by taking wonderful care of her daughter.'

'That's it exactly.' It was a relief to know that he finally understood. 'Bella's my responsibility now. I'm her legal guardian and I love her and I'm committed to watching out for her for the rest of my life.'

Seth nodded. 'It's a big thing to take on. Bella's very lucky to have you.' He looked down at the grass he'd been plaiting and tossed it away. 'I'd like to help, if I can. I know I can't offer much more than financial support. I have to stay here and run this place, but Bella's my family, and she's important to me, too.'

Without warning, he sent Amy a smouldering, half-lidded smile that awoke all kinds of unhelpful memories of last night's kiss.

*I'm an idiot,* she thought.

What was the point of thinking about another kiss when Seth was busily discussing their separate futures?

His thoughts were centred on practicalities, not kisses, and from the start she'd insisted that her future lay in Melbourne with Bella. She'd made it very clear that she wanted to live miles and miles and miles away from here.

Her plans hadn't changed. She couldn't throw them away on the basis of one kiss.

OK, so maybe Seth's kiss had eclipsed all other kisses in Amy's experience, and maybe she was thinking far too much about the chances of a replay, and maybe now that she knew Seth hadn't slept with Rachel, she couldn't think of any reason to say no…

Except…if she was going back to Melbourne, the most she could hope for was a fling. And apparently, Seth didn't do flings. She was pretty sure he was the still-waters-run-deep type of man— which just happened to be Amy's favourite type.

Truth was, she wasn't into flings either, although she believed she could possibly make an exception for Seth Reardon.

Unhappily, she moved to the edge of the rock pool and looked down into the crystal-clear water. She watched the weeds swaying gracefully like thin green scarves anchored to the sandy bottom. She could see the sky reflected in the water and the overhead branches festooned with orchids and birds'-nest ferns like bracelets covering the arms of a belly-dancer.

The bright pink of her T-shirt looked strangely out of place amidst the greens and blues and browns...but as she stood there, watching the reflection, she saw Seth drifting closer, until he was standing right next to her...

Dangerous tingling sensations spread under her skin. She closed her eyes, wishing she could be more sensible about this man. She'd never been forward with guys, but right now she was fighting a shameless urge to turn and throw herself into his arms. *Kiss me, take me...*

'I guess we should go back,' he said, looking down at the water.

Amy let out the breath she'd been holding. 'I guess.'

Seth didn't move...and neither did she.

He was standing so close to her that she only had to sway towards him and their bodies would be touching.

'Amy,' he whispered hoarsely and she saw the movement of his reflection, saw his hand reach out to touch her hair.

When she turned to him, she bumped into his hand. He smiled; let his fingers trace the curve of her cheek, and her pulse began a hectic dance…

'You're so lovely,' he whispered.

*Oh, man.* She was wearing an old T-shirt and jeans. Her hair was in a ponytail and she hadn't a skerrick of make-up. And yet Seth was trembling as he touched her and was telling her she was lovely.

This incredibly attractive, gorgeous man thought she was lovely. This serious man who'd rejected Rachel's flirtations thought she, Amy, was lovely.

In a rocket-burst of confidence and overpowering need, she touched her finger to his lips. 'Just imagine I'm a female firefly and I'm flashing madly,' she whispered.

Seth smiled.

Beautifully.

His kiss started out tender and sweet, but

within seconds it turned earthy and hot. His arms came around her, drawing her hard into his heat.

He broke the kiss for one pulse beat, maybe two…then he began to seduce her slowly, slowly, teasing her lower lip, brushing it with his lips, with his tongue, with his teeth, wringing soft sighs from her, and tiny, tiny moans…before he took the kiss deeper, hungrier, wilder…making her feel like a goddess…

Goddess of the rock pool.

She felt this could go on for ever and getting wilder and wilder, spinning out of control, until she tumbled into the water with him, and swam naked. Made love beneath the waterfall.

'Do you fancy a swim?' Seth murmured into her mouth and his eyes were heavy-lidded and hot as he searched her face.

'You can read my mind,' she whispered, totally, totally lost in longing.

She reached for the hem of her T-shirt and hauled it over her head and Seth groaned softly. His hands were trembling as he touched her breasts.

With a cry, Amy began to tug his shirt free

from his jeans. She'd never been so turned on, so drowning in desire.

But then, at the worst possible moment, like a distant echo from a past life, Seth said one word.

'Bella.'

*What?*

Her mind was too crazed to comprehend. Her eyes were closed, her breath trapped in desperate anticipation of his touch.

'What about Bella?' he said.

Oh, good grief.

She couldn't believe she'd been so carried away that she'd forgotten Bella. Completely.

Seth's groan morphed into a shaky laugh. 'I don't suppose we can leave her with Ming for a little longer?'

A little longer. *How long was that?*

Too long, surely.

*If only...*

With a heavy sigh, Seth gathered Amy close, pressed his lips to her forehead. His hands rubbed her bare arms, muddling her thoughts, making her yearn to throw off her responsibilities.

But how could she be so weak?

She sighed. 'Poor Ming will probably be demented by now. Bella has the attention span of a goldfish. I suppose we'd better head back and rescue him.'

'I was afraid you'd say that.'

His reluctance to leave was flattering, but with a good-humoured chuckle he released her and he bent down and retrieved her T-shirt from the rock at their feet.

He helped her into it, then enfolded her to him one more time, flooding her with happiness.

As they went back along the track and up the stone stairs the wild happiness strummed Amy's nerve endings and she had to stop herself from skipping.

She wasn't sure if this second kiss had been another reckless moment, or the start of something quite, quite wonderful…but exquisite thrills zapped through her like a riff on an electric guitar, and she was too happy to spoil the blissful sensations by analysing them too much.

\* \* \*

Seth watched Amy disappear into the house to relieve Ming of his babysitting duties, and then, as sanity returned, let out his breath on an anguished sigh.

He'd totally lost it, lost himself in the sexy sweetness of Amy's kiss. He'd come within a hair's breadth of dragging her into that pool and taking things beyond the point of no return.

Kissing Amy was fast becoming a dangerous addiction.

But it was madness.

He should never have started this. He should have been stronger, should have had the sense to remember Bella before he made a move on Amy.

He'd set out this morning with the best of intentions, but he'd lost his perspective at some point during the conversation about Rachel and his uncle. He'd kept the details of their story to himself for so long, and it had been damned difficult to talk about what had happened, but Amy had been so incredibly sympathetic, so understanding.

She really did understand. She'd experienced

the same black hole of grief. She'd been living there, in that same painful, guilty place.

She *knew*.

He'd felt a soul-deep connection, and when he'd told her she was lovely, he hadn't only been talking about her dark chocolate eyes, or her lovely smile, or her exceptionally lovely legs. Looking at Amy was a source of constant delight, but he couldn't ignore her warmth and sympathy, or her courage for taking on the responsibility of Bella.

The fact that these qualities all came wrapped in such a sweet, sexy package was a miracle.

Amy had looked so *right* standing there beside the rock pool and he'd almost hoodwinked himself into thinking that she belonged there.

*Fool.*

He shouldn't have started another kiss; should have been stronger. Amy hadn't been flirting. Hell, if she'd been flirting, the kiss could have been excused. But she'd been deadly serious when she'd turned to him.

She'd been asking him to take a leap of faith.

And Seth had no faith.

He'd lost his faith years ago in hard and bitter lessons, and he knew damn well that no amount of loving could overcome the problems posed by this remote lifestyle.

All faith in such rosy dreams had been shattered by his mother, by Jennifer, and by what had happened when Rachel turned up…

Seth's die had been cast then, just as Amy's had. They had separate responsibilities now. He had no choice but to keep Serenity going. He owed it to his uncle to stay here, and Amy had no choice but to return to Melbourne and to raise Rachel's daughter there, surrounded by family, schools, playgroups, ballet classes—everything a little girl needed.

He had no right to dally in kisses, or to toy with Amy's emotions.

For the rest of her stay, he had to remember that. Her sweetness and softness were out of bounds.

Hell, he'd already kissed her twice.

*Twice.*

Two mistakes.

He couldn't afford a third.

# CHAPTER EIGHT

AMY was unhappily aware of how very quiet Seth was as they set off later that morning to explore Serenity in his four-wheel drive.

They were travelling west and ahead of them the sky was leaden and thick with grey clouds. 'Looks like the rain's coming back,' she said.

Seth merely nodded, but she told herself he was concentrating on the narrow, winding track that quite quickly emerged from lush rainforest into open eucalypt bushland and then to grassy plains.

Now, she could see big mobs of Serenity's cattle dotting the wide, flat paddocks. The animals were huge, pale cream and grey with droopy ears and humps on their shoulders.

'What kind of cows are they?' she asked.

'Brahmans. That's the best breed for the tropics.'

'So…do you ride horses and do all those wonderful cowboy stunts?'

'What cowboy stunts?' His eyes held a glint of amusement that suggested he was only pretending to be insulted.

'Oh, you know—throwing a lasso around some poor unsuspecting cow, or turning your horse on a five-cent piece.'

He spared her a small smile. 'You mean the incredibly valuable stock-handling skills that come after years and years of hard practice?'

'Well…yes. Have you been through all the years of practice?'

'Sure.'

'I'd love to see you on horseback.'

She wasn't sure why he frowned. She thought it would be so cool to see Seth thundering over grassy plains after a mob of cattle, or sending water flying as his horse cantered across a creek.

For a short stretch of silence, she let her thoughts play with these swoon-worthy images.

She stole a glance at Seth's jeans-clad thighs, toned from all the hours he'd spent in the saddle, watched the competent way he drove over the rough ground, one hand on the steering wheel, the other smoothly shifting gears.

He was all hard-packed male and capable strength and every time she remembered the way he'd kissed her, the way his hands had touched her, her body caught fire.

Hugging the memories like happy secrets, she dug into her scanty understanding of the cattle industry to find more questions to put to him. When were the cattle mustered? When were calves born and weaned? Were the wet-season floods a problem? How often was a vet required? When did the stock go to market?

Seth answered politely and patiently, but she sensed his cautiousness, too, as if he didn't want to bore her with unnecessary details. His caution bothered her. Couldn't he guess that she would never be bored by anything to do with him? Or his lifestyle?

He pulled up at a group of cottages beside timber-railed stockyards. 'I thought you might like to meet one of the families who live here,' he said.

'I'd love that,' Amy replied with an eagerness that was totally sincere.

Seth frowned and she wondered what she'd said wrong.

Still frowning, he said, 'By the way, these folk know about you and Bella.'

Before she could ask him how much they knew, a tall, rather splendid-looking Aboriginal man came towards them, walking with a long-legged, easy stride.

Seth introduced him as Barney Prior, Serenity's head stockman.

As Amy shook hands with Barney the fly-screen door of the nearest cottage opened and a young woman, willow slender, with arresting green eyes and hair the colour of rich marma-lade, waved to them.

She was wearing a colourful sarong and a sky-blue vest top. Her feet were bare, her toenails painted blue to match her clothes, and a silver chain twinkled at her ankle. Despite her fair complexion, she looked wonderfully at home in this tropical outpost.

Amy liked her at first sight, and her name, she soon learned, was Celia. She was Barney's wife. They'd met in Cairns, they happily explained, and they'd lived together on Serenity station for ten years.

Their two children appeared close behind Celia—a golden-skinned, bright-eyed boy of six and a shy little girl of three.

As soon as Bella was released from her seat belt she shot out of the vehicle like a champagne cork from a bottle. 'Hello, kids! Hello, hello! My name's Bella.'

Luckily the children were charmed by her lavish enthusiasm for their company, and a mutual admiration society was quickly formed.

Within a matter of moments, Seth and Barney were lounging in squatters' chairs on the veranda, keeping watch over the giggling children, who were already climbing the railings on the stockyard fence.

'These guys are going to talk non-stop about

the weather and the condition of the cattle,' Celia told Amy with a friendly wink. 'Why don't we go inside?'

Amy sniffed with delight as she caught delicious smells coming from the kitchen. 'You've been baking.'

'Scones.' Celia laughed. 'I knew Seth was coming.' She glanced at the stove. 'They won't be ready for a few more minutes. I left it a bit late, because I've been busy in the studio. Would you like to see my paintings while we wait?'

For a moment, Amy thought Celia was joking. Uncertain what to expect, she followed her onto a side veranda facing north, enclosed with glass louvres to let in the light. The area was filled with easels and paint pots, and it smelled of turps. Stacked against the inner walls were Celia's paintings.

And. They. Were. Amazing.

Bold, arresting, they completely captured every nuance of the wild beauty of the northern landscape. Amy saw scenes of the open country with straggly pandanus palms, red earth and anthills, scenes of the stockyards, of the main homestead and the gardens, glimpses of the tangled vines, the massive trees and the dark, secret magnificence of the rainforest. And views of the sea.

'These are stunning,' Amy murmured, full of genuine admiration. 'I'm sure they'd fetch a fortune in Melbourne.'

Celia smiled. 'They do.'

'So you've already sold your work?'

'Yes. I've sold several pieces through the Flinders Lane Gallery.'

'Goodness.' Amy laughed. 'Sorry for making assumptions. You're way ahead of me, aren't you?' And then she remembered. 'My friend Rachel brought back fabulous paintings from her trip up this way.'

'Rachel Tyler?'

'Yes.' Amy wondered how much Seth had revealed about her links to Rachel. Celia had shown no curiosity about the sudden arrival of a woman and small child on Serenity. Was she simply being polite?

'Rachel was a terrific help,' Celia said. 'She gave me my best contact down there, and, thanks to her efforts, I made enough money through sales to take the whole family to Italy last wet season.' She grinned. 'Can you believe I did an art course in Florence?'

'How fabulous.'

'I painted to my heart's content, while Barney and the kids ate pizza and gelato and explored the sights. They had a ball.' Abruptly, Celia's smile faded. 'I was so shocked to hear that Rachel died. I couldn't believe it.'

Amy nodded sadly.

'She seemed so happy when she was here,' Celia said. 'She should have stayed.' She shot Amy a rueful smile. 'A car accident. Just goes to show, those cities are dangerous places.'

'They certainly can be.'

Amy almost asked Celia if she was happy living here in a place that had apparently frightened Rachel and would terrify most city women. But she'd already seen the way the other woman's eyes had glowed when she'd exchanged smiles with her husband, and she was sure she knew the answer without asking.

Morning tea was served on the veranda—strongly brewed and accompanied by Celia's scones with blackberry jam and cream.

'Ah.' Seth beamed a blissful smile as he swallowed the last mouthful of his second scone. 'Ming's a genius with a wok, but when it comes to scones he can't hold a candle to Celia.'

Amy bit her tongue before she made a hopeless fool of herself by announcing that she baked quite decent scones, too.

When it was time to say goodbye, Bella cried because she didn't want to be parted from her new friends and Seth took her for a ride on his shoulders to calm her down.

Celia hugged Amy and said how much she'd enjoyed her company. Amy was equally enthusiastic, but when she glanced Seth's way she saw the flare of dismay in his eyes and the sudden tight set of his mouth—and her spirits sank.

It was clear she'd done something to displease

him, and she was terribly afraid he was upset because he'd kissed her. Again.

Big fat drops of rain began to fall as they drove back to the homestead. Amy caught the cindery smell of dampening earth, and wound up her window as the heavy drops splattered the dusty vehicle.

In no time the rain was torrential. Amy had never seen such heavy rain and she had to shout to be heard—and she also had to accept that it was not a good time to tackle Seth about his brooding tension and grimness.

When they reached the homestead, he parked as close as he could to the steps. He unbuckled Bella and took her in his arms as they made a dash through the rain. The distance was short, but they were soaked through by the time they reached the veranda.

Seth's pale blue cotton shirt was almost transparent and when Amy saw the way it clung to his powerful shoulders and chest and his tapered waist, she decided that statues of Greek gods looked weak and flabby by comparison.

It was only when he frowned at her that she remembered her clothing was similarly plastered to her skin.

'I'm sorry,' he said, clearly not pleased. 'I should keep umbrellas in the truck, but we don't have enough female company to remember the niceties.'

'Don't worry about it.' Amy almost snapped at him. Why did he have to look so unhappy about a little wet clothing? Hadn't he been on the brink of diving naked into the rock pool with her this morning?

'I don't need special treatment,' she said stiffly. 'There are lovely thick towels in the bathroom. Bella and I will soon dry off.'

Seth simply gave a curt, worried nod, and excused himself while he went to change into dry clothes, leaving Amy in no doubt that something most definitely had changed between them. The warmth had completely vanished from his eyes.

It was as if they'd never shared kisses, or laughter or painful confessions.

They were back to square one.

As if to confirm this, Seth was polite at lunch

and then he disappeared again, muttering something about having to check beef prices on the Internet. Amy tried unsuccessfully to concentrate on a paperback novel while Bella napped.

When Bella woke the rain was still falling heavily, so they spent the afternoon on the veranda, listening to the steady drumming on the roof, thumbing through picture books, drawing, singing songs and playing hide and seek behind pot plants with Bella's pink pig.

The time was spent pleasantly enough and Amy wouldn't have minded at all, if she hadn't been so unable to stop thinking about Seth.

Try as she might to forget, she couldn't stop remembering the way they'd almost rocketed out of control this morning. The memory of that kiss by the rock pool made waves of longing roll through her, over and over, but it was obvious Seth wanted to pretend it had never happened.

Damn him. Why did he have to be so contrary? He'd been passionate and tender this morning, and withdrawn and moody ever since. Amy wished she hadn't been sensible.

The spell had been broken as far as Seth was concerned, but Amy was still dazzled. All she could think about was Seth and how much she wanted him again. She wanted his kisses, his touch. And if he kissed her again, she wouldn't be sensible.

No way.

There were times when a girl had to throw off responsibility and seize the moment.

By nightfall the rain hadn't stopped.

Bella ate her dinner in the kitchen again and afterwards she demanded that both Seth and Amy tuck her into bed. They took it in turns to read pages from her favourite bedtime book, and they gave her hugs and kisses, but Seth avoided any nonsense about kissing Amy afterwards.

Once again, Ming set the table on the veranda with a romantic candle under glass and floating flowers. The meal was superb—tandoori chicken, accompanied by salsa and a leafy salad, and a crisp white wine. Despite Seth's reserve, Amy couldn't help enjoying the novelty of dining, safe and dry, while the rain streamed past the veranda's wide eaves.

In the dancing candlelight the rain glittered like a silken curtain. Its steady rhythm drummed on Amy's senses. She felt its cool, refreshing breath on her skin, like the gentlest caress of a lover, and she found herself having fantasies about early nights beneath clean, finely textured linen sheets while the weather outside lashed at a dark window.

Of course, the fantasy would be so much more exciting if she weren't sleeping alone...but Seth's increasingly distanced politeness made it patently clear that her chances for romance were dwindling fast.

Seth was struggling.

All day he'd been struggling to put this morning's kiss behind him.

He'd tried to convince himself that he was proud of his restraint, but he was fast losing the battle. Tonight, Amy looked lovelier than ever. Her dark eyes shone in the candlelight and her soft pink dress hugged her figure and made her skin glow. Everything about her filled him with wanting.

As the meal progressed she bravely held up her end of the conversation while Seth did his best to behave like a polite host. He talked about books, and the movies he'd watched on DVD, and he asked more questions about Amy's work in Melbourne.

But he knew he was handling this situation badly. Really badly. And he was pretty sure that he hadn't fooled Amy. There was every chance he'd hurt her.

She was beginning to droop, like a rose in the rain. She didn't finish her food and she drank very little wine. Her fingers twisted the stem of her glass.

*Hell.* He had to say something, do something.

Ming took away the last of their dishes, and they were left alone to finish their wine without further interruption. Seth prised his tongue from the roof of his mouth. 'Amy, I think we should talk.'

Her eyes widened with surprise and a flicker of fear. 'We've been talking all evening.'

Seth swallowed. 'But we haven't talked about what happened this morning.'

The colour drained from her face. 'You wished you hadn't kissed me.'

*Hell, no.* Kissing her was the best move he'd ever made. It was incredible. She'd made him feel like a giddy youth madly in love for the very first time.

But he couldn't tell her that. 'I owe you an apology,' he said.

He saw her shoulders slump and he felt shame in the pit of his stomach. His apology was totally inadequate.

But Amy lifted her chin, as if she'd found sudden courage. 'You're confusing me, Seth. I'm not used to having a man kiss me as if he really likes me, then make me feel like a very bad mistake.'

Oh, God, he deserved this.

'It's not that I didn't want to kiss you. You must know that.' He dragged in a breath, forced himself to add, 'But I shouldn't have allowed it to happen.'

To his surprise, she narrowed her eyes at him

and dropped her head to one side, watching him shrewdly.

'OK,' she said slowly. 'Tell me one thing. Why *did* you kiss me?'

It was a fair question, but for the life of him Seth couldn't think of a fair answer—not with Amy sitting there, looking like every kind of temptation he'd ever known. There was only one reason he'd kissed her. He'd wanted her, wanted her so badly he hadn't been able to think of anything else.

But he had to get his mind past all that now.

As if she'd guessed he wasn't going to give a straight answer, she let out a soft sigh. 'You know, there are all kinds of kisses, Seth. From my possibly limited experience, I know there are hello kisses and pleased-to-meet-you kisses, and I'd-like-to-do-that-again kisses.'

A deep pink blush crept into her cheeks and she dropped her gaze to the bowl of frangipani. 'And then there are kisses like your kiss this morning.' Her blush deepened. 'I've never been kissed like that before.'

She glanced up quickly and he saw the silver glitter of tears in her eyes and his heart felt as if it had shattered like glass.

'You kissed me as if you were making love to me. You showed me exactly what it would be like if you made love to me. And I'm afraid I haven't been able to think about anything else, ever since.'

*Oh, Amy, Amy, Amy.*

He couldn't bear that he'd hurt her…. She was so courageous and honest…and *lovely*.

If he thought he could make her happy, he would do so in an instant.

But if he weakened now…if he gave in…everything he'd been trying to protect would be destroyed. In a heartbeat he and Amy would be down the hallway and in his bed together, making fabulous, amazing, heartbreaking love. He would be lost in this sweet, courageous girl's kisses. His hands would be caressing her soft, smooth skin. Her lovely, warm body would be linked with his.

He wanted all of it. All of her. Now. He wanted to inhale her, to know every part of her intimately, to bind himself to her.

He'd spent three days battling this desire, and for Amy's sake he had to be strong. She wasn't a girl to be trifled with and he had to resist this last, terrible test.

'I'm sorry you feel that way,' he said, hating the lie, but knowing it had to be said. 'I gave in to an impulse when I should have known better.'

A tear spilled down her cheek and she hastily dashed it away.

*Don't touch her.*

Clenching his hands into tight fists, Seth said, 'I don't want to mess things up for you, Amy. You came here to find Bella's father, not to get involved with me.'

She took a small sip of wine as she considered this. After a bit, she said, 'Are you scared I might get too serious?'

'Perhaps,' he admitted reluctantly. 'I certainly don't want to send you back to Melbourne with emotional baggage. You have Bella to worry about. You don't need complications.'

'Why does a relationship have to be complicated?'

Something as hard and as spiky as coral lodged

in Seth's throat. 'Our situations were already complicated, even before I kissed you. We're from two completely different worlds.'

She sat very still, as if she was thinking this through, and Seth prayed that she understood.

After the longest time, she shrugged her shoulders. 'You're scared I'll fall in love with you.'

'And vice versa,' he whispered.

Her mouth titled in a slow, knowing smile. 'I don't know, Seth. I think you're making a mountain out of a molehill. If you're worried about kissing me, maybe it would help if I kissed you instead.'

He tried to cover his groan with a laugh. 'How will that help? We'd both be in trouble.'

Clearly she wasn't put off. Her smile lingered. 'Wouldn't it be the honest way to find out what's going on between us?'

'Amy, don't play games.'

'Games?' Her smile faded. Painful seconds rode by, then she gave a bewildered shake of her head, let out a noisy sigh. 'OK, I'll behave, but I think you owe me a better explanation than that.'

\* \* \*

So they ended up on the sofa, not in bed, as Amy had hoped. She sat sedately at one end, with her skirt smoothed over her knees, and Seth sat a discreet distance away from her, with his long legs stretched in front of him, crossed at the ankles.

With a theatrical flourish, she positioned a row of red and purple striped cushions between them. 'That's the no-go territory, right? It'll save us both from these complications you're so worried about.'

He smiled wryly.

OK. Problem was, now she'd got this far, she was so nervous she thought she might be sick. Had she really asked Seth Reardon to explain exactly why he couldn't risk falling in love with her? Did she need this depth of pain and humiliation?

She couldn't believe she'd been so pushy. The tropics must have melted her common sense.

'What exactly would you like me to explain?' he asked.

At that very moment, Amy wanted to turn tail and run. But where would that leave her?

A nerve-jangling wreck.

'I guess I'd like to get everything straight in

my head,' she said. 'It seems we've both more or less agreed there's a mutual attraction, but you're saying we shouldn't do anything about it because—'

She nodded to him to take over.

'Because I live alone at the end of the earth and you live in Melbourne in the bosom of your family, with a great job and a small child and—'

'Wait a minute.' She made a sweeping gesture that took in the length of the lovely veranda. 'What if I actually liked this particular end of the earth?'

Seth rolled his eyes. 'You'd soon get sick of it here.'

'Other women live on Cape York.'

He didn't respond immediately, but she saw a flash of hurt in his eyes and she guessed.

She forced herself to ask. 'Is that what happened to the girl who—who broke your heart?'

After a beat he nodded. 'She went home for a short stay and never came back. She came to her senses instead.'

'But you really loved her?'

'I'd asked her to marry me. We were engaged.'

So, yes, he'd really loved her. Amy's throat tightened painfully. 'Where was her home?'

'New York City.'

A low whistle escaped her. 'Serenity would certainly be a culture shock for a girl from New York.'

'No more than it is for you, or for Bella,' Seth said tersely.

'Are you saying this is no place for a woman? Or there's no place for a woman in your life?'

He let out an impatient sigh. 'Look, I'm not warning you off because I'm still nursing a broken heart. This isn't about me and my tender ego. It's about trying to protect you. It wasn't easy for Jennifer to call off our engagement. She had a kind of breakdown. It was a really bad time for her.'

'I'm sorry.'

Amy's throat ached as she tried to hold back tears. She could feel the other woman's pain, as if it were her own. It would have been beyond terrible to have loved Seth, and to know that he returned her love, that he wanted to marry her, and then to discover, too late, that she couldn't cope with his remote lifestyle.

This Jennifer must have been devastated to give him up.

'Jennifer did the right thing, Amy. She knew she wouldn't be happy living here for ever.'

'Is she happy in Manhattan?'

'Married with two children the last I heard.'

He looked so grim Amy wondered if he was still in love with Jennifer. If that was the case, she also wondered why he hadn't thrown off his responsibilities here and gone after her.

She supposed the very fact that he hadn't gone showed how deeply he was anchored to this place.

But was he right? Couldn't a woman be happy here? The right woman?

She remembered the pain in Rachel's eyes when she'd talked about Bella's father. *I couldn't live there. It's so hot and wild and remote—I'd drive the poor man insane.*

Problem was, Amy couldn't really understand why Serenity was such a problem for Jennifer, or for Rachel. It was remote, sure. Seth had already explained that, and she'd seen for herself how long it had taken to drive from Cairns to Tamundra, and then from Tamundra to here.

But Seth flew a plane, and there were other people living here, and the house and gardens were absolutely beautiful…and if a couple really loved each other…

'What about Celia?' she asked.

Seth frowned. 'What's Celia got to do with this?'

'She lives here. Barney's house is just as remote as yours, and it isn't nearly as big or comfortable as your place, but Celia's blissfully happy.'

'Celia's different.'

'Of course she is. Everyone's different.' As Amy said this, she had a sudden burst of clarity, as if a knot in her thoughts had untangled. She wanted to punch the air in triumph. 'Seth, that's the point you're missing. You can't assume that every girl will be the same as Rachel and your American fiancée.' More gently, she added, 'Or your mother.'

She squeezed a smile. The logic of her argument seemed perfect to her, but after a stretch of silence Seth shook his head.

'Celia grew up in Far North Queensland,' he said. 'Coming here wasn't such a big change for her.'

Amy let out a heavy sigh. It was like talking to a brick wall and she had a terrible feeling that she could talk all night and not change Seth's mind. Even if she ripped off her clothes and lured him into bed, he would still want to send her back to Melbourne. The knowledge that he wasn't going to change sank inside her like a lead weight.

'OK,' she said softly. 'I've said my piece. Maybe I should shut up now.'

To her horror, her eyes flooded with tears.

*No. Please, no. Don't let me cry. I have to retain a shred of dignity.*

Quickly she jumped to her feet. 'You didn't ask for me to come barging up here, and I seem to be making life very difficult for you.'

When he didn't deny this, she cast a despairing glance at the rain. 'I'm sorry.'

Still he didn't speak and Amy couldn't bear to look at him.

'If the weather's not too bad in the morning,

I'd be grateful if you'd take me back to Tamundra first thing,' she said, and, without waiting to see if he planned to respond, she turned and hurried away.

# CHAPTER NINE

AMY slept in and when she woke she was groggy-headed and exhausted after another agonisingly restless night.

The first thing she remembered was asking Seth to take her back to Tamundra today, and she was swamped by a cold wave of misery. Oh, God. How could she feel so lost-in-a-black-hole dreadful over a man she'd known for a few days?

Desperate to feel better, she sat up quickly, and saw that Bella's bed was empty, just it had been yesterday.

But this morning Amy refused to panic—she knew Bella would be safe, playing with Seth in his room. Each day, the little girl was becoming more and more infatuated with him.

*Funny about that.*

Amy indulged in a huge yawn and slowly swung out of bed. She shuffled her feet into slippers and yawned again as she opened the wardrobe to get out her dressing gown. For once, she would be covered up when she said good morning to Mr Reardon.

The rain had stopped and the world outside was strangely quiet, but when she listened more carefully she could hear the now familiar birdcalls and the peep-peep-peeping of the tree frogs. She brushed her hair, tightened the knot in her dressing gown and went into the hallway and called to Bella.

There was no answering call from Seth's bedroom.

Amy winced. After last night's unhappy 'discussion', the last thing she wanted was to come face to face with Seth's bare chest and his pyjama bottoms, but she had to make sure Bella was safe.

Gingerly, she tiptoed forward. 'Bella, are you in there?'

Again, there was silence and another step showed her that the room was empty.

Amy stared at the huge unmade bed and

rumpled sheets. Bella's pink pig was lying on the carpet beside the bed and Amy's heart swooped painfully. Where were they?

She told herself she wasn't going to panic. She'd slept in quite late, so Bella and Seth had probably started their breakfast without her. Tugging the lapels of her dressing gown higher, she went down the hall to the kitchen, and found Ming putting the final touches to a fruit platter.

He turned and grinned at her. 'You've had a good sleep in.'

'I hope I haven't held everyone up?'

He shook his head. 'You're the first to show up for breakfast.'

'Really?' She tried to ignore a spurt of fear. 'Where are Seth and Bella?'

Ming frowned. 'Seth's down at the hangar, checking over the plane.'

'The plane?'

'He said something about flying you to Cairns today.'

Oh, yes, he would want to get rid of her by the fastest means possible, she thought unhappily.

'I thought little Bella was with you,' Ming said.

Now tendrils of true fear snaked around Amy's heart. 'I haven't seen her. She's not in our bedroom, and I've already checked Seth's room. Do you think she could be at the hangar with him?'

'I'd be surprised.' Ming frowned. 'But I guess it's possible. There's a phone line to the hangar. I'll give him a call.'

'Thanks. While you do that, I'll start searching the rest of the house.'

Stomach churning, Amy went to the veranda first, checking behind furniture and pot plants and under the dining table in case Bella was playing hide and seek.

From the veranda railing she looked down into the fenced pool area, and was relieved to see that it was empty.

She was determined to remain calm and she went back to the bedroom she shared with Bella and checked beneath the beds and in the wardrobe. She checked the bathroom, then Seth's bedroom and bathroom, where she caught a lingering waft of his aftershave. Bella wasn't there.

In the hallway, she met Ming, looking worried. 'Seth hasn't seen Bella,' he said. 'He's coming back to the house straight away.'

'Have you checked any other rooms?' She was beginning to feel frantic now.

'I've checked my room and the study and the laundry,' Ming said.

'What about the pantry?'

'Yes, I've had a good look in there. No luck, I'm afraid.'

'I'll check the gardens, then.'

Amy began to run and every fear she'd ever felt in her life paled into insignificance compared with the terrible, suffocating fear that filled her now. She couldn't lose Bella. She simply couldn't.

She mustn't.

'I'll send Hans to start searching out the back,' Ming called after her.

Heart in mouth, Amy flew down the steps. Bella couldn't have disappeared. She had to be all right. She just *had* to.

'Bella!' she called as she rushed along wet

paths between plants and shrubs still drooping after the rain. 'Bella, where are you? Come on, sweetie, it's time to stop hiding now.'

She kept telling herself that she would hear Bella's giggling laughter very soon now. She would find the little girl toddling up a pathway, grinning happily, arms outstretched.

As she rounded a tall hibiscus bush, however, it wasn't Bella she ran into, but Seth.

'Hey,' he said, gripping her arms to steady her. His blue eyes pierced her as he searched her face. 'You haven't found her yet?'

Amy shook her head and her mouth turned square as she tried not to cry. 'I slept in, and by the time I woke up she was gone. I thought she was with you. Her toy pig's in your room.'

He shook his head. 'I was up very early.'

'She must have gone looking for you, then. I don't know where she is.'

'Don't worry,' he said gently, and he pulled her against him and hugged her and she felt his heart beating hard above hers. 'She can't have got far. We'll find her.'

'She's so little,' she whispered, and to her horror she remembered the pythons out in the rainforest. Oh, it was too hard to be brave.

'I'll find her, Amy,' Seth murmured, and he pressed a warm kiss to her cheek. 'I promise.'

For a brief, thrilling instant, his big hand cradled her head against his shoulder and she closed her eyes, absorbing his strength and the musky warmth of his skin, the laundered cotton of his shirt, and she felt suddenly, wonderfully reassured.

'You should wait at the house,' he said as he released her. 'Bella might turn up there at any moment. Don't worry, Amy. Barney's on his way. He's a brilliant tracker, and Hans and Ming are already searching. We'll find her.'

'Good luck,' she whispered as she watched his retreating figure, tall, broad-shouldered, lean-hipped. Competent…

As Seth hurried away his stomach was in knots. Sweat trickled down his back, and his mouth was dry as bulldust.

He was facing terrible truths he hadn't fully ac-knowledged till this moment. He loved little Bella. Deeply, painfully.

She wasn't simply a cute, sweet, baby girl— she was his flesh and blood. His family. The daughter of the man he'd loved as a father.

And—he'd fallen in love with Amy…

The savage, inescapable truth tore at his heart.

Amy didn't deserve this worry. She'd turned her life upside down for Bella, and it was only because of Bella that she'd made this long journey north. He'd do anything to banish the awful fear from her eyes.

He'd told Amy that he'd find Bella and, by God, he would. He'd move heaven and earth to return the little girl safely into Amy's arms.

But the child was so tiny and this place was so wild, and he was gripped by the worst kind of terror.

Amy went back to the veranda and sat on the top step, hugging her knees. She tried to pray, but her fear kept getting in the way.

She kept picturing Bella's cheeky smiles and dancing blue eyes, kept hearing her high-pitched voice singing off-key, kept remembering the joy of Bella's little arms hugging her, the softness of her skin and the sweetness of her baby kisses.

How had she actually thought she could let her feelings for Seth get in the way of her responsibilities to Bella? How could she have been so sidetracked last night? So selfish?

Oh, heavens. Was Seth right when he'd said this was no place for a woman, or a child? There were snakes here, and crocodiles and dark, dangerous forests and—

She would go mad sitting still.

She jumped to her feet and began to pace. Appalling horrors crept into her thoughts, but she fought them back. She wouldn't allow herself to think the worst. There were four experienced men out there searching for Bella. The child was only two, and she had little short legs. Seth was right; she couldn't have gone far.

Could she?

She reached the end of the veranda for the third time, turned around for the third time, and was about to pace back when she heard a cry.

'Cooee!'

Her heart leapt.

Running to the top of the steps, she heard another cry. It was Seth's voice and he sounded elated, but she couldn't make out the words.

Heart pounding, Amy gathered her dressing gown around her knees and flew down the steps, then dashed across the lawn in the direction of the voices.

Seth and Barney were coming towards her.

She saw a bundle in Seth's arms.

'Hi, Amy!'

Bella's voice called to her in the bright, happy, eager and innocent way that she greeted everyone.

With a sob of joy, Amy stumbled towards the little group and there were hugs all round, for Bella, for Barney, for Seth.

Seth's face was alight with laughter and Amy could sense his deep joy and relief, but when she looked into his eyes she saw something more—

the dying glimmer of terror and pain and fear, mixed with a tenderness that pierced her heart. She burst into tears.

Breakfast was something of a celebration.

After Amy washed her face and changed into a T-shirt and jeans, she joined the others on the veranda. She was embarrassed by the way she'd cried all over Seth, but he'd been very sweet about it, offering her his handkerchief, and stroking her hair and trying to cheer her up by explaining that Bella had strayed only a little way down the main track.

Apparently, Bella had decided to go looking for 'the kids', as she called Barney and Celia's two youngsters.

Now there were six on the veranda for breakfast—Barney and Ming and Hans, as well as Seth and Bella and Amy.

The men ate their way through a mountain of bacon and sausages and eggs, and they laughed and joked and fussed over Bella. Everyone, especially Seth, was trying to make light of the mishap now, but Amy knew she could never forget how horribly close they'd come to tragedy.

And sadly, Bella's misadventure had proved Seth right.

If ever there was an experience that proved they didn't belong here, this was it. She and Bella had caused all sorts of disruptions, and she didn't want to put any of these men through that level of worry again.

She accepted now that it was time to go.

All too soon, breakfast was over and Barney, Ming and Hans were heading off to work.

'I should say goodbye to you now,' Amy said, forcing a smile.

The men looked surprised. Ming sent a concerned glance in Seth's direction, but it was Barney who spoke. 'You're leaving already?'

Amy nodded, and avoided Seth's eyes. 'I'm afraid I have to get back to work, too.'

It should have been gratifying that these men appeared genuinely sorry to say goodbye, and Amy held onto her smile as she thanked them all again for their help in finding Bella. Hans offered to take Bella for a ride in his wheelbarrow, and he promised to keep a close eye on the little girl while Amy packed.

Seth waited until only he and Amy were left on the veranda before he said quietly, 'You know you don't have to rush away today.'

'But I think it's best, don't you? As long as it suits you to fly today, of course.' She turned to him and was dismayed by the bleak and lonely shadows in his eyes.

He looked so sad, and she thought, for one tingling, breath-robbing moment, that he was going to beg her to stay.

But almost immediately his air of sadness was replaced by nonchalance, and he shrugged. 'I've checked over the plane and the airstrip. It's not too boggy, and the sun's out now, so it should be fine for take-off.'

'What about the hire car I've left in Tamundra?'

'I'll get one of the men to run it down to Cairns when the rain stops.'

'Thank you. I guess I should pack, then,' she said in a small voice.

'Take your time,' Seth said coolly. 'There's no rush.'

But Amy had to rush. Her nerves were too frayed—she had no choice but to dash about her room, hunting for Bella's toys and books, folding clothes, slipping spare shoes into bags and swiftly stacking them into their suitcases.

If she stopped for a moment she might think.

She didn't want to think.

She'd done too much thinking here, and now it was time to hurry away before her mind—or her heart—imploded.

They set off midmorning, flying south into another bank of cloud. The hum of the motor and the steady vibration of the plane soon made Bella drowsy. Amy closed her eyes, too, and pretended to sleep.

It was cowardly, perhaps, to avoid conversation with Seth, but she was afraid she would become terribly emotional, and blurt out something that would embarrass them both.

Closing her eyes didn't help, of course. Her mind kept going over and over the events of the last few days. She couldn't believe it had been such a short time. She'd been through so much. She remembered her first meeting with Seth in the Tamundra pub, remembered the way Marie, the publican's wife, had warned her about him.

*Eyes that make you wonder…*Marie had said, and, oh, boy, was she right.

Amy flashed to their first night here at Serenity when she'd told Seth that Bella was Rachel's daughter, to the fireflies in the heart of the rainforest, that one deliberate stroke on her hand, the meals on the veranda, the kisses… Oh, dear heaven, the kisses…

And then, this morning's drama.

Her chest ached when she remembered the depth of emotion she'd seen in Seth's eyes when he'd brought Bella to her, and the ache became unbearable when she thought about the sadness and loneliness she'd witnessed as well.

She'd wanted to throw her arms around him, to hold him and to tell him that it didn't have to be this way.

He could have them.

She and Bella would stay if he asked.

But she knew he wouldn't ask. He'd been through enough tragedy. He wasn't taking any more risks.

It was still raining in Cairns.

Apparently, it had been raining for days, and a blustery wind swept in from the sea, making Amy's umbrella difficult to control as they ran across the tarmac in the general aviation area.

Seth had rung ahead and secured seats for her and Bella to fly direct to Melbourne, and they would be home by teatime.

Home. Already, Melbourne no longer felt like home.

With Seth in charge, everything proceeded like clockwork. He accompanied Amy and Bella to the domestic terminal, checked in their baggage and got their boarding passes.

He was especially attentive to Bella. When she spied a toy 'rocking' plane, he put two dollars in a coin slot and gave her a ride, and stood watching her with a smile that didn't quite reach his eyes.

He took them to a café and ordered apple juice and a cookie for Bella, and coffee with biscotti for Amy and himself. He was going out of his way to be helpful and Amy lost count of the number of times she said thank you.

Apart from thanking Seth, she said very little. Her tiredness and the aftershock of this morning's crisis had taken their toll, and now the knowledge that very soon she would walk out of Seth's life brought her to the edge of tears. It was far safer not to speak…

And yet as she watched Seth entertain Bella with a magic thumb-sliding trick she knew there were things that needed to be said.

'Bella's going to miss you,' she told him.

He shrugged. 'Little kids have short memories.'

'I wouldn't bank on that, Seth. She's a bright little button. Besides, I won't let her forget you. You're her family.'

'She'll have you.'

Amy knew the flippancy in his voice was forced. He was putting on a brave face, pretending a coolness he didn't feel.

'Your family can provide her with all the aunts and uncles she needs,' he said. 'Grandparents, cousins. What more could she want?'

'A father.'

He scowled and shook his head. 'You know that's not possible.'

'But you've become her father figure, Seth. You're important to her, even after such a short time.'

His response was a sharply indrawn breath.

'I plan to keep in touch.' Amy wasn't sure how she managed to keep talking without breaking down. 'I—I'll make sure you don't miss the milestones.'

'When's her birthday?' he asked.

'March the fourteenth.'

He nodded and Amy watched a cold shadow of sadness slip over his face.

'But there'll be other milestones, Seth. Starting kindergarten, school, learning to play the cello.'

His eyebrows rose sharply. 'Cello?' For a scant moment, he almost looked amused.

Amy shrugged. 'Cello, ballet, pony club… Whatever. She's bound to have interests.'

'Yes,' he agreed quietly.

'As I said, I'll keep in touch.' Now her voice was definitely very scratchy and choked.

'You do that,' he said, 'and I'll come down for the special occasions.'

'Or I can bring her back here.'

'It's probably better if I come down. It would be too disruptive for you to try to come all this way.'

She suppressed an unhappy sigh.

'You'll send me a copy of Rachel's book, won't you?' he said.

'Yes, of course.' As she said this Amy realised with a nasty jolt that everything else that had happened had pushed Rachel's book clear out of her thoughts. She shook her head at him. 'Don't look so worried, Seth. I'm sure we can trust Rachel.'

Too soon, their flight was being called for boarding. The shimmer in Seth's eyes and the determined set of his mouth made Amy's throat ache more painfully than ever.

What was there left to say? *I've had a wonderful time* was pitifully inadequate.

Seth carried Bella to the boarding gate and he cracked a crooked smile as he rubbed his nose against hers.

Amy looked at the narrow walkway leading to the plane. Passengers were hurrying along it, eager to be on their journey. But they were going to something, looking forward to their destinations, whereas Amy could only think that she was leaving. Going away. For ever.

Unable to hold back the impulse, she said, 'You know, you could always put a fence around the homestead.'

The words tumbled out.

Seth looked stunned, and she felt foolish, but she was about to walk out of his life, so she had nothing to lose.

'If you want to keep a child safe, all you have to do is put up a fence around the homestead,' she told him. 'Serenity could be as safe as a house in the suburbs.'

For a scant second Seth's eyes flashed with a

hopeful light, but it disappeared so quickly Amy wondered if she'd imagined it. He shook his head and his smile was a happy-sad mix of amusement and despair. 'Amy, get on that plane.'

He gave Bella a kiss and then set her down, and as Amy took her chubby hand she was grateful that the little girl couldn't really understand the concept of goodbye.

Seth's eyes glittered too brightly. Amy felt the heat of his skin as he leaned close. She felt the warm pressure of his lips, just once on the corner of her mouth.

'That kiss was goodbye and it was very nice to know you,' he said softly.

Her eyes stung and her throat was so painful she could scarcely speak.

She couldn't bear this. How was it possible to fall so deeply and completely in love with a man and still walk away from him?

'One last thing, Seth.' She tried for a smile and missed. 'Just remember that we're not the ones who are dead. We still have long lives to live. You, me and Bella.'

And then she turned, showed their boarding passes to the waiting flight attendant, and she held Bella's hand very tightly as they went through the exit doors.

# CHAPTER TEN

AMY tried to convince herself that she and Bella were better off in suburban Melbourne with its rows of safe brick cottages behind neat brick fences. She knew she should feel secure and reassured by the familiar sights of Melbourne's trams and skyscrapers, and its umbrella-carrying businessmen in dark, serious suits.

Here in this great southern city the gardens were pleasantly tidy and manicured and the grass didn't grow six inches overnight. The hedges here were soft green, carefully clipped and well behaved.

Now that she was safely back in Melbourne she could put the lush and shiny extravagance of the tropics out of her thoughts. She could slowly forget the spicy fragrance of ginger flowers and cardamom, the delicate scent of frangipani.

And surely, in time, she would stop thinking about a tall, rangy cattleman who wore battered jeans and faded shirts, and who strode through the tropical rain without a coat or an umbrella.

Like Rachel, she would put those heady days she'd spent in the tropics down to experience. She would get on with the life she was meant to live, in the south, in the city that was famous for having four seasons in one day, rather than long, intense and endless summers and glorious, balmy non-winters.

She told herself that she'd been happy enough before she set off for the north and she could be happy again. She'd find fulfilment in her work, in taking care of Bella. She and Bella would once again be a special little unit, facing the world together.

Who needed guys anyway? Dominic and Seth had used up every last drop of her romantic blood. She was over men. From now on, the most important days on her social calendar would be Bella's play dates and her family's get-togethers.

After all, she'd only known Seth for four days, so this ghastly gaping hole inside her couldn't possibly be love. If she distracted herself with hard work and with taking very special care of Bella, the wound would eventually heal.

At least that was the theory.

Six weeks later, however, as Amy organised the finishing touches for Rachel's book launch she still felt a painful, distressing longing for Seth Reardon and it remained lodged in her heart like the dart of a poisoned arrow.

Seth stalked Amy's thoughts during the day and she dreamed about him every night. His name was a constant ache in her throat. She'd lost weight and people—notably, her family— were beginning to worry about her.

Her mother tried to talk to her about it and Amy would have liked to pour her troubles into her mum's sympathetic ear. Really, she would have spoken up, but she'd known Seth for such a short time she was sure her mother wouldn't believe that she could possibly know him well enough to truly love him.

Anyone with common sense knew that you needed time to get to know a man properly before you could be sure you loved him.

Until she met Seth, Amy had been brimful with common sense, but now it seemed to have deserted her. Common sense couldn't explain the deep, shattering yet exhilarating certainty that her life belonged with Seth Reardon.

There were times when Amy thought about that other woman—Seth's fiancée, who'd gone back to New York and found she couldn't give up her lifestyle. Amy wished she could find the same certainty and security in Melbourne. She wished she could feel that she would, in time, be cured of Seth, but she feared it was impossible.

She blamed herself for losing him. She'd been too pushy, asking far too many probing questions.

In her stronger moments, she was determined to be stoic about the whole thing, to stop being selfishly maudlin and to be grateful that Bella had one important link to her flesh-and-blood family.

During this time, there was only one good piece of news. Rachel's book turned out to be a lovely, heart-warming romance, and, as Amy had expected, it was beautifully written. Rachel had used her poetic skills and sensitivity to perfectly capture the story of a couple falling in love in the tropical north.

She'd made the world of Cape York come alive on the page, and as Amy read late into the night she could once again see the tapestry of the clouds, the movements of the butterflies, the strident colours of the parrots and the flowers. She could smell the rainforest, could hear the bird-songs, feel the tinkling crunch of coral underfoot.

But while Rachel's setting was authentic, her characters bore no resemblance to the people who'd lived on Serenity.

For one thing, their love story ended happily.

Amy sent a copy to Seth and included a note to say that she hoped he was as pleased as she was that his family's privacy had been respected. She was disappointed, but not surprised, when Seth didn't reply.

It was patently and painfully clear that he was determined to keep his distance.

* * *

Seth dreamed of Amy.

Together, they were hosting a party at Serenity and the verandas were filled with the sounds of their friends' laughter and a jaunty jazz CD playing in the background. Children were running on the lawn. Bella was there, as well as Barney's two, and another little fellow, a chubby toddler. In the dream, Seth had been sure the child was his son and he'd felt a rush of astonishing love and tenderness for the cheeky little chap.

He woke to the smell of burning gum leaves, rolled in his swag and squinted through the creamy dawn. Barney was crouched over a small fire, using his Akubra hat to fan it to life. Soon the billy would be boiling and they would make tea. They'd fry up a couple of snags and toast slices of bread over the coals. Before the sun was properly up, they'd be in the saddle again, continuing their cattle muster.

It was time to shake off the lingering effects of the dream and his restless night—*another* restless and miserable night.

Seth rose and stretched his arms high, then bent

down and fished his wristwatch from inside one of his dusty riding boots, the safe spot where he kept it every night when he was out in the bush.

In the faint early light, the watch glinted as he slipped it over his wrist, and he found himself suddenly staring at it as if he'd never seen it before.

The metal band was unnecessarily fancy and he hadn't bothered for years with adjusting the intricate dials that simultaneously told the time in two parts of the world.

Why hadn't he noticed before that out here in the bush, surrounded by red dirt, anthills, straggling pandanus and mobs of cattle, the watch looked totally wrong? It was too citified, like the woman who'd bought it for him, a relic from an unhappy past.

'Why am I still wearing this thing?' he muttered out loud.

Hell. Only a fool carried a constant reminder of unhappiness. All the time he'd worn it he'd been blinkered, with his eyes fixed on everything that had gone wrong in his life.

*Crazy.*

Seth took the watch off again and hooked it on a tree branch while he rolled up his swag. After breakfast, he and Barney watered their horses, loaded their saddle packs and stamped out the fire. With luck, they'd have the mob back in the home paddocks in two days' time.

'Hey,' Barney called as Seth swung one leg high over his horse's back. 'Don't forget your watch.'

Seth looked back and saw it hanging on the branch, gleaming like a weird kind of Christmas-tree ornament, and he shrugged. 'You want it?'

Barney frowned, rode over to the tree, and snagged the watch. 'What's the matter with you? You're not going to leave this here, are you? It must be worth a bit.'

'Maybe your young Sam would like it,' Seth said. 'He's old enough now for a watch.'

Barney sent him a puzzled smile. 'Sam would love this, but why? What's got into you?'

Seth grinned at him. With a flick of his reins, his horse took off in a canter and he called over his shoulder. 'Maybe I've come to my senses at last.'

\* \* \*

Amy's close links to the author and her background in marketing made her the perfect choice
to organise the launch of *Northern Sunsets*, and
she worked on the fine details with the publishers and the bookstore proprietor to make sure it
was a huge success.

The launch was to be a Friday-evening cocktail
party in a trendy bookstore in the heart of the
city. Huge posters of the book's stunning cover
and a portrait of Rachel, looking gorgeous and
Bohemian, had been hung from the ceilings.

A display filled a big front window with the
photos Amy had taken at Serenity as well as
books, and there was also a tiered stand of books
just inside the store's entrance. A barman had
been hired to serve cocktails with tropical names
such as Mangolicious, Coral Sea Breeze and
Pineapple Passion.

Amy had almost given in to the accepted law
that black was de rigueur for a cocktail dress in
Melbourne, but at the last minute she scoured
boutiques until she found a cute strapless number

in coral pink. She added silver sandals and a frangipani behind her ear.

When she looked in the mirror, she felt a catch in her breathing. She was back on the veranda at Serenity, where a table was set with bamboo mats, and a candle beneath a glass cover. Flowers floated in a pink bowl and the fragrant smell of simmering curry drifted from the kitchen.

When she closed her eyes, she could hear Seth's footsteps coming towards her, could feel the brush of his lips on the nape of her neck, and the thrill of his arms enfolding her.

*Yeah, right.*

She shook her head to clear it of the nonsense. Each day she was a step closer to getting over Seth Reardon. OK, so maybe she still had a few thousand steps ahead of her before the mission was accomplished, but his continuing silence left her with little choice. She was determined to move on. If it killed her.

On Friday evening, Amy stood to one side of the main display and watched with growing delight as the shop filled with booklovers enticed by the ads she'd placed in the media. There weren't going to be any follow-up books, so it was really important that this launch went well. The publishers were super keen for *Northern Sunsets* to sell squillions.

Amy allowed herself one sad moment, when she fervently wished that Rachel could have been there to enjoy the glory and the fame and excitement that was due to her, but she couldn't afford to think about that for too long, or she'd be a mess. Anyway, despite Rachel's outgoing nature, she'd never liked to big-note herself.

Once Amy was sure that everything was going to plan, she began to circulate, smile pinned in place, chatting with enthusiasm. At first, when the woman she was talking to appeared a little distracted, she took no notice. She was trying to describe her initial impressions of Cape York.

But then the woman said, 'Oh, my! Does that man know you?'

'What man?' Amy turned to follow the direction of the woman's gaze.

'The tall fellow there with the amazing blue eyes and—'

Amy didn't hear the rest.

Her ears had filled with the deafening roar of her galloping heartbeats.

Seth.

Was here.

He was standing alone, dressed like every other man in the room, in a conservative dark suit with a white shirt and dark tie, but even in city clothes he was stop-and-stare gorgeous. All sorts of people were turning to take a second look at him, almost as if they thought he was a celebrity they should recognise.

Across the busy bookstore he sent a smile to Amy, and she felt her eyes well with tears. He began to thread his way through the sea of people, and she wasn't sure her legs would support her.

Dimly, she was aware that the woman she'd been talking to muttered something about getting a drink.

And then Seth was standing in front of her.

He was smiling as he greeted her. 'Hello, Amy.'

It was a moment or two before she could speak. 'Hello,' she said at last and she was shaky and nervous and breathless all at once. 'What—what a surprise.'

His smile deepened, making beautiful creases in the corners of his eyes. 'It was a spur-of-the-moment decision.'

'So you got the book I sent?'

He nodded. 'I found it yesterday when I got back from mustering. It was in the pile of mail.'

'Mustering?'

'We've been rounding up the cattle after the wet season, and I've been out bush for quite a few weeks.'

Well, of course it made sense, didn't it? She hadn't seen Seth working with his cattle, so she hadn't given them a second thought, but now she was ridiculously pleased that he had such a credible reason for not writing back to her.

She wanted to stare and stare at him. He looked so wonderfully refined and handsome in his suit. She loved the way his collar sat so neatly against his suntanned neck, loved the way his shoulders filled his jacket so beautifully. Compared with the city fellows with their pale complexions and pudding-soft stomachs, he carried an indefinable air of belonging to a different breed.

He'd come all this way.

Why?

At last she remembered her manners and she held up her cocktail glass. 'Would you like a drink?'

Seth cast a dubious eye at the contents of her glass, the colour of a tropical sunset.

'Not now, thank you.' And then he asked, 'How's Bella?'

'Oh, she's fabulous. She's talking in proper sentences now, and I can't shut her up. She loves learning new words. Her latest is upside down.'

Amy knew she was gabbling, but Seth was making her dreadfully nervous, even though he looked genuinely interested in hearing about Bella.

The bookstore was filled to capacity now and people were squeezing past them, holding their drinks high so they didn't spill.

'How did you know about this launch?' she asked, lifting her voice above the buzz of conversation.

'You sent a brochure.'

'Oh, of course.' She'd sent him all the promotional material with the book, as a courtesy. And here he was twenty-four hours after receiving it.

Nervously, she asked, 'So…what did you think of the book?'

'It's very good. Not the sort of thing I usually read, but I was really impressed.'

'You must have been relieved to see that the characters were entirely fictitious.'

'Absolutely. I must admit I feared the worst.' His mouth twisted in a self-deprecating smile. 'Seems I was brewing a storm in my own teacup.'

Amy let this pass. 'I thought the descriptions were fabulous. The landscape seemed so real.'

Seth nodded. 'Rachel certainly had a gift.'

She drew a quick breath. All week she'd been talking intelligently to strangers about the book, but now, with Seth, it was suddenly difficult.

She tried again. 'Most people I know have loved the ending.'

As soon as she said this she winced. How crass could she get? The book's ending was wonderfully happy and romantic. Why had she mentioned it to *this* man?

She was shaking.

Seth was looking directly into her eyes. 'The ending's perfect,' he said.

The warmth in his smile melted every bone in Amy's body and she was in danger of dissolving into a puddle on the bookstore's carpet, but she was saved by a loud tap-tap-tap on the microphone.

'Excuse me, ladies and gentlemen. Can I have your attention, please?'

It was time for the formal speeches, and the buzz in the room died.

Amy found a place to set her drink down and she took several deep, steadying breaths, bracing herself for the bittersweet emotions that always came when tributes were paid to her friend.

As Rachel's talent was praised in glowing terms Amy was grateful for Seth's tall, strong presence beside her. After the first speech, Rachel's literary agent, her publisher, the bookstore owner, and a librarian all wanted their five minutes in the spotlight, and although Amy tried, *really* tried to concentrate on every word, her mind buzzed back to her unanswered questions.

Why had Seth come? *Really?* Why was he smiling at her so—so warmly?

As soon as the speeches were over, he jumped in with questions of his own.

'What are your commitments here, Amy? Do you have to stay till the bitter end? Do you need to help with stacking things away?'

Dazed, she shook her head. 'Why do you ask?'

'I was hoping we could slip away.'

Her heart did a backwards somersault.

'I'd like to talk, Amy.' His smile wavered.

'Talk?'

As she watched him his face changed. His smile slipped away and his features grew tight and serious. For a moment, his eyes had that shadowy, hopeless look that she'd seen on that final morning at Serenity, and it scared her, because she didn't know how to make it go away.

'I'd like to talk about us,' he said. 'Unless I've frightened you off completely, and you'd rather not.'

She pressed a hand to the leaping pulse in her throat and told herself that she mustn't read too much into this. 'I—I think it would be OK to leave now. I just need to say goodbye to a couple of people.'

Rachel's agent accepted Amy's apology with a knowing wink. 'I can't blame you for wanting to run away with that man.'

Amy pretended she hadn't a clue what she meant.

The other woman smiled. 'Off you go, honey. Run, before someone else nabs him. He's frighteningly gorgeous.'

Amy went.

Outside in Bourke Street the air had quite a nip and she drew her shimmering silver pashmina around her.

Seth eyed it with concern. 'Will those cobwebs keep you warm?'

'Oh, yes,' she assured him. 'This is cashmere.' As she said this she realised that a shrewder woman might have been less honest, so that Seth felt compelled to put his arm around her.

Then again, how could she be sure that Seth wanted to put his arm around her? He'd made it very clear that he wasn't looking for romance. Not with her, at any rate.

But he wanted to *talk* and she was almost sick with worry. What if he didn't plan to tell her any of the things she needed him to say? What if she was misreading his sudden appearance in Melbourne completely? She so wanted him to tell her that he'd missed her, but she was equally scared she'd make a fool of herself.

His gaze flashed down to her high-heeled silver sandals. 'I don't suppose you'll want to walk too far in those glass slippers.'

She gave a shaky laugh. 'They're not too bad, actually. I can manage a couple of blocks.' After all, she thought, it might help her to calm down if they walked while they talked. 'Would you like to go down to the Yarra River?'

'Yes. Good idea.'

Together they set off, with Amy's high heels clicking on the concrete, while Seth measured his steps to match hers.

'How long will you be staying in Melbourne?' she asked.

He sent her a tense smile. 'For as long as it takes.'

She stumbled and his hand gripped her elbow. 'Careful, there.'

For as long as *what* took? She was too nervous to ask.

'How have you been, Amy?' His voice sounded strangled and tight.

'I've been very well, thanks. Life has been good.'

Seth shot her a sharp glance. 'Is that an honest answer?'

In spite of her warm wrap, Amy shivered. 'I'm not sure you'd want honesty.'

'But I do.' His eyes were deadly serious. 'I want to know exactly how you feel.'

*Exactly…*

The fierceness in Seth's eyes told her that this was important.

*Oh, boy.* Amy took a deep breath. If she was going to be exact, she would tell Seth that she'd missed him every minute of the past six weeks. She would tell him that she'd almost been flattened by heartache. But she'd exposed her feelings to this man before, and he'd rejected her soundly.

If she sacrificed her pride again she feared she might not recover.

She also knew, however, that if she tried to lie, her face would give her away.

'Well, if you must know,' she began bravely, 'I've been trying very hard to get over you.'

'Have you been successful?'

'I thought I was making reasonable progress.'

In the light cast by an overhead lamp she saw the jerky movement of Seth's throat, and wondered if he felt as she did: as if he were walking along a knife edge.

'What about you?' she asked. 'Why have you come here, Seth?'

'I had to see you, to see if you were OK now.'

'Do you mean you wanted to reassure yourself that I like being back in Melbourne? Were you expecting me to be relieved now that I'm safely away from you and Serenity?'

He stopped walking. Amy stopped, too, and they stood facing each other.

A group of young people went past, couples arm in arm.

'Don't you like being back in Melbourne?' Seth asked.

'Not especially.'

His intense blue eyes searched Amy's face, but he didn't speak and that maddened her. She knew there were very good reasons why he doubted her—his mother's defection, Jennifer's rejection, Rachel's denial of his uncle. But why couldn't he believe she was different from those other women?

Amy might have set him straight, might have told him that Melbourne wasn't much fun when she was pining to be somewhere else, but to confess that was like launching off a cliff into thin air. How could she be sure Seth was ready to catch her?

Tears burned her eyes.

'Amy,' Seth said softly. 'Can't you guess?'

She blinked. 'Guess what?'

'How much I've missed you.'

He took another step towards her and his eyes shimmered. 'Saying goodbye to you at the airport was the most painful experience of my life. The minute you'd gone, I knew I'd done the wrong thing.'

He gave her a sad, lopsided smile. 'I thought going away on the cattle muster would help. It would give me some distance and I could get my head straight. But each night, as soon as the work stopped, all I could think about was you.'

Amy felt her mouth wobble, as if she was trying to smile, but she was still too scared, too terrified that she might be dreaming this.

'I wanted to rush down here and sweep you off your feet,' Seth said, 'but I knew it wouldn't be fair to you.'

'Because I might have already lost interest in you?'

'Yes,' he admitted unhappily. 'But then I

realised I had no choice. I had to come and look you in the eyes and ask—'

The entire city seemed to stop as the air solidified around Amy.

'I wanted to ask how you feel now about—' Seth swallowed '—about everything.'

'Everything?'

'Me. Serenity.'

'Oh.' A fat tear spilled onto her cheek. 'You're an impossible man.'

Seth stood very still, eyes too shiny, throat working, then he smiled shakily and held out his arms to her.

Next breath, they were together, clasping each other tightly. 'Amy, Amy... Amy.'

She was laughing and crying.

Seth kissed her cheek and then her eyelids and he wiped away her tears with his thumbs. He drew her into the alcove of a shopfront so he could kiss her properly.

*Oh, man.*

When they'd been at Serenity, Seth had told her that he couldn't risk another kiss, but now he was kissing her as if his life depended on it, and Amy knew, deep in her heart she could tell…

He was risking all that he had.

Later, much later, they pulled apart, but only a little apart.

'So…' Seth looked happy as he touched her cheek. 'Where's this river of yours?'

'Oh, it's just another block away.'

'Let's go there.'

Linking arms, they began to walk on, past shops with beautifully lit window displays, which Amy couldn't normally resist, but this evening blissfully ignored. She still wondered if her feet were actually on the ground. She was sure she must have been visibly glowing.

At the pedestrian crossing they waited impatiently for the lights to change, and ahead of them lay the Yarra River, dark and silent, gleaming like an unrolled bolt of black satin.

'This is more like it,' Seth said when they reached the bridge.

It made perfect sense, she thought, that even in

the middle of a big city like Melbourne Seth sought out a river, the one natural element amidst all the concrete and steel and glass. They stood together, forearms resting on the bridge's smooth stone balustrade, watching the way the lights from the buildings on the Southbank made fat yellow stripes on the dark, silky water.

Amy remembered another time when they'd stood together, looking out at the sparkling Coral Sea while they shared heartbreaking confessions. It was the morning she'd decided that she loved this man, and in that moment her love had felt like a beautiful gift, something bright and wonderful resurrected out of tragedy.

For the past six weeks she'd tried to tell herself that she'd been wrong—foolishly so— but now Seth was here, miraculously, beside her in Melbourne.

She had to ask. 'You said you're here for as long as it takes. What do you mean? As long as *what* takes?'

He gave her a tender smile and touched the

frangipani behind her ear. 'As long as it takes to fix the damage.'

'Damage?'

He traced the curve of her cheek. 'I hurt you, Amy. I know I did.'

She couldn't respond without crying, so she bit her lip.

Seth said, 'I was holding back from you, because I didn't want to start something, only to end up hurting you. But then I watched you walk onto that damn plane, and I knew that I'd hurt you anyway. So I'm here to make amends, to try again.'

A cool breeze rippled the water's surface, bringing a faint smell of mud, and breaking up the stripes of light on the water. The wind played with Amy's hair.

Seth leaned a little closer. 'I mean it, Amy. I don't think you've any idea how much I've missed you.'

He looked serious and scared, and Amy loved him for it.

'Probably not as much as I've missed you,' she said.

He reached for her hand, enfolding it in his warmth.

'If it's OK with you, I'm not planning to hurry away.'

'That's very OK,' she assured him. 'How long can you stay?'

Seth shrugged. 'I've left Barney in charge at Serenity. He's breaking his neck to have a crack at running the place.' His face broke into a grin. 'I should be honest and tell you that everyone's missed you and Bella—Ming, Hans, Barney, Celia and the kids.'

He chuckled softly. 'As soon as I got back from the muster, they were pestering me blind to know when you're coming back to Serenity.'

'What did you tell them?'

'That I was going to Melbourne to ask you that very question.' Seth drew her into his arms and his warm lips grazed her jaw.

A delicious shiver scampered over her skin.

'You're cold,' he said.

'Just a little.'

'Let me take you somewhere warmer.'

Amy said softly, 'Perhaps you could take me home.' A bright blush flared in her cheeks. 'So you could see Bella,' she added, 'although she's sound asleep.'

She watched the slow unravelling of his smile.

'I'd love to see Bella,' he said.

And just like that, holding hands and laughing, they ran as fast as Amy's high heels would allow to the nearest taxi rank.

From the tiny front porch of Amy's flat, they watched the young babysitter safely negotiate the footpath and turn in at her gate two doors away.

Amy had to pinch herself. She still couldn't quite believe that Seth was here in her flat—all six feet plus of him, looking gorgeous in his dark suit, and quite possibly planning to stay the night.

'Bella's this way,' she whispered.

Light from the hallway spilled into the small bedroom, illuminating the sleeping child. Seth stood behind Amy and they both looked down at Bella's dark ringlets, at her eyelashes curling like black little commas against her flushed pink cheeks, at the familiar fat pig clutched in her chubby hand.

'My uncle would have loved her,' Seth whispered, and his voice was rough around the edges.

Amy swiped at her eyes with the backs of her hands as Seth followed her outside into the hallway.

Reaching for her wrists, he drew her close enough to kiss her damp cheeks. 'The thing to remember is that Bella's a very lucky little girl to have you, Amy.'

Gently, his hands cradled her face and he smiled into her teary eyes. 'Let me tell you something a very wise woman once told me.'

'What's that?' she sniffled.

'You and I are the ones who still have lives to live.'

Her heart seemed to swell inside her as Seth's lips traced a dreamy path over her jaw. 'Do remember telling me that?'

'Of course.'

'Ever since, I've been thinking about the way I want to live the rest of my life.'

'H-have you found an answer?'

'I'm working on it.' He rubbed his lips softly against hers and she thought she might explode with wanting him. 'That's why I'm here,' he said. 'I was hoping maybe we could work something out. Together.'

Now she was smiling. In fact she was grinning so hard she thought her face might grow stretch-marks. 'That sounds like a plan.'

# EPILOGUE

THE trail of frangipani and gardenia petals was Hans's idea. The flowers led along the garden path and up the steps to Serenity's big veranda, where the wedding would take place.

For many weeks Hans had spent every waking moment working hard to make sure that Serenity's garden was at its best. Now, pots of romantic, trailing wisteria adorned the veranda. Chinese paper lanterns glowed warmly in the grape-purple twilight, and the romantic strains of a string quartet drifted into the gathering dusk.

Flowers trailed along the edges of the long trestle tables that would soon groan beneath the weight of the fabulous food that Ming and two friends from Cairns had prepared.

Wedding guests were gathered on the veranda, talking in hushed whispers.

At a nod from the visiting bush padre, Seth, who was waiting in the wings, turned to his best man. 'That's our cue, mate.'

Barney's white teeth flashed in his dark face as he grinned. 'I've been waiting a long time for this day.'

Minutes earlier, Celia had pinned tiny orchids on their lapels and told the men they looked 'seriously dashing' in their dark formal suits.

Now, the men stepped together onto the veranda, and there was an audible collective gasp. Seth smiled at his guests—at Amy's family, at Celia and her children and the various friends from both Melbourne and the Far North. They'd all been accommodated right here on Serenity, either at the homestead, or in the stockmen's quarters.

'Hi, Daddy,' called Barney's little daughter, and everyone laughed, breaking the tension.

The padre, the same sympathetic and worldly-wise man who'd come here to bury Seth's uncle, smiled at Seth now, then he gave Seth a kindly wink. 'Your bride is on her way.'

*Your bride.*

The two words set off happy explosions inside Seth.

Amy, his bride, his warm-hearted, lovely bride, his friend, his lover was coming to him.

Truth be told, she was only coming from the back of the house, making her way on her father's arm, through the garden, following the trail of flower petals, but Seth was impatient to see her.

Over the past three months they'd spent as much time together as possible. In Melbourne they'd enjoyed trips to the theatre, and to restaurants. They'd taken Bella to the zoo, and the three of them had driven up to the Dandenong mountains for picnics.

They'd spent a weekend at Queenscliff, enjoying the cold southerly sea breezes as much as the seals and fairy penguins. Seth had been to dinner with Amy's parents, and to a Ross family barbecue, where he'd been given the once-over by Amy's brothers and apparently had passed muster—no easy thing to achieve.

Back on Serenity, both Amy and Bella had started riding lessons. Amy was keen to learn every last thing about Seth's cattle business, and she'd hatched all sorts of exciting plans.

Each day, Seth had grown happier and surer that he and Amy and Bella were meant to be together as a little family, and he'd felt the certainty and rightness take root deep inside him.

Now, his heart gave a lift as he saw Bella coming along the path that wound between the shrubs and ferns. Her dark curls shone in the light of the lanterns and her dress was of palest pink tulle, and she looked like something from a fairy tale. His smile widened as every so often she stopped to pick up flower petals, which she solemnly placed in the tiny white straw basket she carried.

Behind her, in elegant pearl-grey silk, came Amy's bridesmaid, Jane, and then, on her father's arm, was Amy.

Misty-eyed and smiling Amy.

Beautiful in white.

Seth remembered the first time he'd seen her in the Tamundra pub, hurrying after Bella, and his heart gave the same unexpected lift he'd felt that day.

Now she reached him, and with a smiling nod her father stepped back.

Amy slipped her arm through Seth's and smiled at him. He smelled the delicate scent of the flowers in her bouquet, saw her love shining in her warm, dark eyes and he was terrified he might cry with happiness.

'Hi, Sef,' called a small voice.

He looked down and there was Bella, reaching up to hold his free hand.

To have and to hold.

Seth grinned, and Amy laughed, and he felt his tension melt away.

The ceremony began, and the reassuring clasp of a small, warm and slightly sticky hand remained with Seth as he and his bride promised to be together for ever.

**MILLS & BOON PUBLISH EIGHT LARGE PRINT TITLES A MONTH. THESE ARE THE EIGHT TITLES FOR JULY 2010.**

———————— ❧ ————————

## GREEK TYCOON, INEXPERIENCED MISTRESS
Lynne Graham

## THE MASTER'S MISTRESS
Carole Mortimer

## THE ANDREOU MARRIAGE ARRANGEMENT
Helen Bianchin

## UNTAMED ITALIAN, BLACKMAILED INNOCENT
Jacqueline Baird

## OUTBACK BACHELOR
Margaret Way

## THE CATTLEMAN'S ADOPTED FAMILY
Barbara Hannay

## OH-SO-SENSIBLE SECRETARY
Jessica Hart

## HOUSEKEEPER'S HAPPY-EVER-AFTER
Fiona Harper

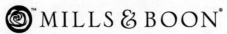

0710 Rom LP

# MILLS & BOON PUBLISH EIGHT LARGE PRINT TITLES A MONTH. THESE ARE THE EIGHT TITLES FOR AUGUST 2010.

## THE ITALIAN DUKE'S VIRGIN MISTRESS
Penny Jordan

## THE BILLIONAIRE'S HOUSEKEEPER MISTRESS
Emma Darcy

## BROODING BILLIONAIRE, IMPOVERISHED PRINCESS
Robyn Donald

## THE GREEK TYCOON'S ACHILLES HEEL
Lucy Gordon

## ACCIDENTALLY THE SHEIKH'S WIFE
Barbara McMahon

## MARRYING THE SCARRED SHEIKH
Barbara McMahon

## MILLIONAIRE DAD'S SOS
Ally Blake

## HER LONE COWBOY
Donna Alward

MILLS & BOON

WEB/M&B/RTL2 LP

*Discover Pure Reading Pleasure with*

## Visit the Mills & Boon website for all the latest in romance

**Buy** all the latest releases, backlist and eBooks

**Find out** more about our authors and their books

**Join** our community and chat to authors and other readers

**Free** online reads from your favourite authors

**Win** with our fantastic online competitions

**Sign** up for our free monthly eNewsletter

**Tell us** what you think by signing up to our reader panel

**Rate** and review books with our star system

# www.millsandboon.co.uk

 Follow us at twitter.com/millsandboonuk

 Become a fan at facebook.com/romancehq

L.T.
HANNAY,
BARBARA

PORTSMOUTH PUBLIC LIBRARY

3 3230 00627 1724

AUG
DAT

PRINTED IN U.S.A.

GAYLORD

PORTSMOUTH PUBLIC LIBRARY
601 COURT STREET
PORTSMOUTH, VA 23704

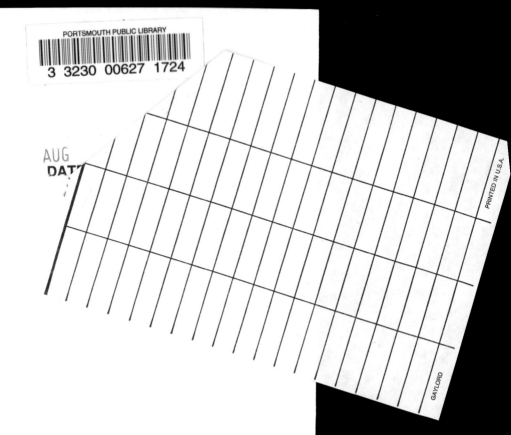